She wanted to freeze the moment and stay in it forever, where she wouldn't have to make impossible decisions.

But she had to stop it. If even contemplating selling the Hideaway to him wasn't betrayal enough, wanting to kiss him would stamp a seal on her treachery that would stay with her forever.

But before she could push him away, his hands closed around her upper arms. She felt dizzy and confused for a moment, and then the world stopped spinning in circles and snapped back into brutal focus.

What was she doing, standing ankle-deep in freezing water, wanting to kiss her worst enemy? She pulled away and stepped backward, but he kept a light hold of her.

"I thought you were going." The chill of the water had spread through her whole body.

"I will go just as soon as I'm sure you aren't going to fall over into the sea."

"Why would I do that? I'm perfectly fine." She shivered violently.

He lifted one shoulder, a wealth of expression in the spare movement, and then dropped his hands.

"You're sure you're alright?"

Dear Reader,

During countless holidays in Cornwall, I have dreamed of living there in the place that has enchanted me through all seasons and all weathers.

Cassandra Greenwood has never dreamed she would call anywhere else home. For generations, her family's roots have been buried deep in the foundations of the Cornish Hideaway Hotel.

But now she is being forced to sell the Hideaway to her worst enemy.

Matheo Chevalier's plans to make the staff redundant and redevelop the hotel are unbearable, and so Cassandra strikes a deal with him. But she soon discovers that working with Matheo is much more than she bargained for, and her heart is in far greater danger than the old building.

If Cassandra loses both her home and her heart to Matheo, what can the future possibly hold for her?

Cornwall's rugged cliffs, battered by the westerly seas, its hidden coves and secret creeks hold an irresistible wildness and mystery. This story has been shaped by those landscapes and by an ancient granite building that has crouched atop the cliffs for centuries.

In reading this book, it is my hope you will fall in love with Cassandra and Matheo's story, and with Cornwall, too.

Suzanne

Off-Limits Fling with the Billionaire

Suzanne Merchant

ISBN-13: 978-1-335-73711-3

Off-Limits Fling with the Billionaire

For questions and comments about the quality of this book, please contact us at CustomerService@Harlequin.com.

Harlequin Enterprises ULC
22 Adelaide St. West, 41st Floor
Toronto, Ontario M5H 4E3, Canada
www.Harlequin.com

Printed in U.S.A.

Suzanne Merchant was born and raised in South Africa. She and her husband lived and worked in Cape Town, London, Kuwait, Baghdad, Sydney and Dubai before settling in the Sussex countryside. They enjoy visits from their three grown-up children and are kept busy attempting to keep two spaniels, a dachshund, a parrot and a large, unruly garden under control.

Books by Suzanne Merchant

Harlequin Romance

Their Wildest Safari Dream

Visit the Author Profile page
at Harlequin.com.

With thanks to Sue and Geoff, on the
Roseland Peninsula, for the years of friendship
and warm hospitality that continue to nurture
my love affair with Cornwall.

CHAPTER ONE

'CASS? CASS, where are you? There's a man in the garden, and he's… What are you doing?'

Cassandra gripped the ladder and balanced the broken piece of plaster cornice across the top of it. She shuffled her feet until she could perch on the second step from the top. If she ducked her head, she could see a slice of the view.

The sea sparkled, blue and silver. Above it, clouds raced across the pale spring sky. It was her favourite view in the world. It could soothe fears, calm tempers and bring her that sense of home that she treasured above all else.

Except soon it wouldn't be her view any more. The realisation that this was probably the last time she'd see it hit her like a physical blow that threatened to expel the air from her lungs and stop her heart in mid-beat.

She twisted her head, dragging her eyes away, and looked down at Tess, her PA, instead.

'Last-minute repairs,' she said through gritted teeth. 'This bit fell off again last night.'

'Perhaps you should come down…'

Cassandra wished she'd been more honest with the staff of the Cornish Hideaway Hotel. She'd told them she'd been forced to sell, but she knew she'd been too upbeat when she'd described her plan to persuade the new owner, whoever that might be, to retain the staff.

Tess clutched a chipped mug of coffee in one hand and bit into the flaky Danish pastry she held in the other. She looked up at Cass again and her eyes widened in surprise.

'Cass? You look…different.'

For a horrible moment Cass thought Tess was going to choke on that mouthful of pastry, adding manslaughter to her own personal list of crimes. Deception, and deliberately ignoring hard facts when they were staring you in the face were two of the others she could think of.

But Tess gulped and swallowed a mouthful of coffee.

Cass squirmed.

'How did you get your hair to do that? And are you wearing make-up?'

Cass put a hand on the neat knot at the back of her head, checking it was still intact. She'd secured it with proper hairpins and half a can of hairspray, but its defiance of gravity still seemed miraculous. She shrugged.

'Hairspray actually does what it says on the

tin. I think it's really wallpaper glue in a spray-on formula.'

'You look pale. Have you had any breakfast?'

'It's the make-up. And I didn't sleep that well last night.'

She had hardly slept for a week. Not since the lawyers had said she had no option but to accept the offer she'd received for the Cornish Hideaway Hotel. It wasn't high enough to clear the debts but, as they'd pointed out, with each day she delayed those debts would continue to mount.

And then, early this morning, they'd let her know about a new possible buyer. She'd breathed a sigh of relief, not because she hoped for more money—there was scant hope of that—but because it meant she could delay her decision by another twenty-four hours, at least.

'Why,' asked Tess, brushing flakes of pastry off her shirt and onto the floor, 'have you put your hair up and put on make-up?'

'There's someone else coming to look at the Hideaway. He's booked in to stay the night. I need to look business-like. I'm going to change…'

'That must be who I saw, and I don't think you have time to change, but you can probably sneak a coffee in, if you're quick. *He* was talking to George in the garden. He's *divine*-looking.' She rolled her eyes. 'Who is he?'

'The CEO of a company called Marine Developments. That's all I know.'

'I think George was bending his ear about never having enough time to grow his vegetables because of all the running repairs he has to carry out on the building, but he looked really interested even though he was probably bored...'

Cassandra shook her head. The mere thought of coffee—of *anything*—made her stomach heave.

She straightened her knees and inched around again, wishing she'd changed before tackling this job. Wishing she hadn't seen the broken cornice at all, wishing... Wishes were a waste of time and energy. And anyway, they never came true.

'I must get this done,' she muttered. If only Tess could stop talking to her, just for a minute, and let her concentrate.

She yanked the claw hammer from the waistband of her jeans and propped the ancient piece of moulded cornice in place. Squinting, she aimed a vicious blow at the rusty nail protruding from one end of it.

'Oh, Cass, he's...'

'Ow! *Crap!*' The hammer clattered to the floor and the cornice flew through the air. Cass sucked her injured fingers and squeezed her eyes shut, instantly losing her balance. She swayed, lost her footing and slithered down the ladder, into the arms of the man she had vowed she never wanted to see again.

'Merde!' His voice was deep, with the hint of a Gallic accent. 'What the *hell* are you doing?'

Cass stared up into grey eyes, stormy with annoyance, and the memory swamped her. The firm yet gentle grip of his hands on her upper arms felt oddly familiar, even after so many years. And his eyes held the same steeliness, except anger had replaced the concern they'd held back then. For one insane moment the essence of his strength almost overwhelmed her, and she thought how easy it would be to surrender to it; to lay her head on his broad chest and let someone else take the strain.

She dismissed that madness, placed her hands instead of her cheek on his chest and pushed herself away from him. He let go of her arms, massaged his shoulder and nudged the offending piece of cornice out of his way with the toe of a polished leather shoe.

He would have had to duck through the door, she thought, even though it was one of the newer doorways, built to an almost twenty-first-century height. He ran a hand through his windswept dark hair and glanced around the room, and then his gaze returned to her face.

Cass stepped backwards until she felt the ladder behind her. She raised her chin a fraction and took a deep breath, hoping the hammering her heart had set up in her chest would steady. But as long as those implacable eyes held hers, she knew she had a snowball's chance…

The suit he wore screamed 'bespoke', or, more

likely, *fait sur mesure*. The words were probably stitched into the lining. Beneath the jacket and crisp white cotton shirt his body looked—*felt*—hard and toned. As rock-solid, she was willing to bet, as the business deals he and his father struck.

In the fourteen years since their last, brief meeting he had been transformed from a twenty-something diffident young man, obscured by his father's shadow, to a thirty-something fully-fledged, independent powerhouse. She'd hoped—*prayed*—that the sale of the Hideaway would escape the notice of the formidable Chevalier clan. How naïve was that?

He stopped rubbing his shoulder and extended his right hand. His fingers were long and bronzed, the nails squared off and expertly manicured.

He had no right to be early; to catch her unprepared. The business suit she'd brought down from London last week was useless , hanging behind the door of her attic bedroom. And right now she could have done with the extra inches a pair of heels would have given her.

'Miss Greenwood.' All trace of annoyance had been wiped from his eyes and his voice. His tone was even. 'Shall we start again and renew our acquaintance in a more civilised way?'

His gaze drilled into her and she knew she had to return it or betray her confusion. Mesmerised by the sheer force of his confidence, Cass put out her hand. He flexed his cool fingers around hers and she wished her palm wasn't damp with anxiety. He'd notice, of course. He wouldn't miss a thing. Her hand was trapped, just like the rest of her, but if she hoped to save any of her self-respect, she needed to break the contact between them.

His presence and his utter self-assurance were intimidating. From the arrogant tilt of his head as he surveyed her study, to his faintly dismissive expression, it was obvious that Matheo Chevalier did not doubt himself. He might as well have spoken the words out loud. He was about to gain control of what he and his family had wanted for so long.

She opened her mouth, but he spoke first.

'We met once before.' Her hand was still in his. 'I came here with my father, but you probably don't remember. You must have been…about sixteen?'

Cass remembered. It wasn't a time she'd ever been able to forget. She remembered the sense of desperation that had gripped them then. She and her father, crushed by grief, struggling to come to terms with the changed order of things. Despite all the treatments the doctors had tried, all the money her father had spent on futile attempts to halt it, the disease had claimed her mother's life with cruel speed.

Cass had felt as if she'd been cast adrift on an alien sea with no familiar landmarks to navigate by, dreading the next blow but not knowing from which direction it would come. She'd clung to her father; he'd always known what to do. He'd been the rock on which she and her mother had depended. His solidarity had been unquestionable.

But she'd quickly discovered he was no longer the father she recognised. He'd become unreachable, engulfed in grief so intense that he seemed to have to expend all of his energy on keeping it locked inside him. Cass became afraid to talk to him, afraid of what might happen if he allowed any of it to escape.

Within a few weeks the next blow had materialised in the form of the rich, successful hotelier Charles Chevalier. He'd wanted to buy the hotel, pointing out that he was willing to pay over the odds for what was, by rights, his property anyway. Joe Greenwood would be able to settle his debts, he had said, contempt in his tone, as if he was doing them a favour, trying to force them to part with the home they loved.

Matheo Chevalier had retreated from the argument that had erupted between the two older men. After his weeks of silence, Cass had felt an odd sense of relief that her father could still string a coherent sentence together. But then she'd listened, shocked, as, in language more colourful than anything she'd ever heard, he'd declared he'd sell his soul to the devil before he sold the Hideaway to a lying, cheating Chevalier.

Fast forward fourteen years, and here was the son, hiding behind a different company, about to try again.

She pulled her hand from Matheo Chevalier's, memory stoking her anger. He might be smooth-talking, but he was his father's son, and she wasn't going to forget it.

He'd tried to be kind to her during the few frightening, confusing days of their visit. He'd asked about her mother, and she'd attempted to describe the dark, bottomless pit of sorrow that yawned inside her. He'd lost his mother, too, he'd said, when he was ten, and then he'd been sent away to boarding school, where he hadn't been allowed to be sad.

They'd walked on the beach, climbed on the rocks, and talked. It had been cathartic for Cass. She had told him of her fear of the future, of how she sometimes thought she heard her mother's voice and how her father had become a stranger who had decreed that nothing in the hotel could be changed. Nothing at all.

And if he was his father's son, she was her father's daughter. Old grievances ran deep.

'I remember you.' Her voice surprised her with its firmness, considering how wobbly she felt. She remembered how she'd reacted when he'd first tried to talk to her, the mix of fear and betrayal of loyalty to her father. 'But I remember your father better.'

'And I remember yours,' he responded, drily. 'I'm unlikely ever to forget his opinions of my family, or his lack of restraint in expressing them.'

'My father never believed in mincing his words, and he had scant regard for moral weakness.'

'Which he considered my father to have in spades.'

'And your grandfather, too.'

His laugh was low. 'You've changed in the past fourteen years. I remember you as something of a wild child. And fragile.'

His eyes travelled over her, and she hoped he saw that the wild child had been well and truly banished. Any latent wildness had disappeared for good that day a year ago, when her father had died, shockingly and suddenly, leaving her with nothing but the almost unbearable responsibility of saving the hotel and preserving the livelihoods of its faithful staff.

As for fragility, she'd shed that, too. What didn't kill you made you stronger, and she had survived. The years of coping with her father's descent into depression, forcing herself to leave him to go to college, forging a career for herself in the competitive world of interior design and surviving the break-up of a controlling relationship had transformed her into a stronger woman than she'd have believed possible back when she'd first met Matheo Chevalier.

If she'd seemed wild, it had been wild with grief, perhaps, or maybe fear at what the future could possibly hold without her mother to keep her safe.

'You've changed too. You were the only person I'd really spoken to in weeks, and you seemed to understand.' She shook her head. 'But it seems you've assumed the family mantle with enviable ease. And you have a new company name. Did you mean to take me by surprise? To catch me out?'

His eyes darkened, slate hard, and his mouth, which had softened as he studied her, compressed into a straight line.

'Yes,' he said. 'I have changed. And Marine Developments is a company that was set up two years ago. It's not exactly new.'

'Your father, I remember, has always got what he wanted. He's played a long waiting game.' She shrugged. 'But I'm afraid you may be too late. I'm about to accept an offer.' Suddenly the too-low bid seemed attractive, if it meant not selling to the Chevaliers, but she knew her lawyer would not share that view.

'Naturally you are free to sell to any of the other bidders.'

Cass was not free at all. She'd be pressured into taking the highest offer, and quickly, and she was sure he knew that. The knowledge would be giving both him and his father enormous satisfaction.

'But your position is very weak. It would be sensible to go for a straightforward sale to the highest bidder.'

Cass didn't want to be sensible. She wanted to keep her home, and the staff, some of whom had known her all of her life, around her, so that all the memories of her parents and her childhood would not be obliterated by the plans of a mega-successful property developer.

'Selling at all is a betrayal of my father's wishes. I will never compound that by selling to the Chevaliers.'

Matheo Chevalier slipped a leather bag off his shoulder and put it on the desk as if he already owned it. He turned and strolled over to the window. 'My interest in the Hideaway has nothing at all to do with my father.'

'You expect me to believe that?' Disbelief coloured her voice. 'Your grandfather and then your father used every means available, some definitely unscrupulous, to try to get control of the Hideaway. Don't tell me this has nothing to do with the past.'

Cass looked past him, towards the sea. White caps had appeared, foaming on the crests of the waves as they rolled into the cove below. The wind must have changed direction, she thought absently. She tried to focus on what he was saying, through the fog of despair that engulfed her at the thought of finally leaving this place, with its ever-changing weather but never-changing comfort of home.

She'd spent the whole of the past year trying everything possible to keep the hotel going, but when the accountants had presented her with the bald financial facts she'd been forced to accept that selling was unavoidable. At least this way she'd be able to pay most of the outstanding bills. And if she used the full powers of her persuasion with the new owners, some of the staff might keep their jobs.

'I would like to have found a way…' She hated the defeat she could hear in her own voice.

She brushed a cobweb from her jumper and glanced down at her faded jeans and scuffed trainers. How could she expect anyone to take her seriously, dressed like this?

From the corner of her eye she caught a movement, and she swung her gaze back into the room. Tess, whose presence she'd completely forgotten, was sidling silently towards the door, her eyes huge with surprise.

'Tess, wait…' she called out, desperate to offer an explanation, though she didn't have the faintest idea how to phrase it. The long-standing feud between theGreenwoods and the Chevaliers was the stuff of legend at the Hideaway, along with the myth of the treasure, reportedly to have been smuggled out of France by the Chevalier ancestors, on the run from the Revolution and a date with Madame La Guillotine. Now the identity of the latest prospective new owner was going to get out in the worst possible way. She had no reason to believe Tess would be discreet. She'd be bursting to tell everyone what she'd heard.

'Tess!'

Matheo's voice, like a blade sheathed in velvet, carved through the silence and Tess, who had ignored Cass's plea, froze.

'Tess,' he repeated, a fraction more softly. 'Could you organise some coffee for us, please? There are points I need to discuss with Miss Greenwood.'

Cassandra watched as Tess struggled to respond. She looked like a mouse caught in the mesmerising stare of a cat. Then she ducked her head and swallowed.

'Coffee. Yes...of course.' She backed towards the door. 'Mr Chevalier, sir.'

His laser gaze flicked back to Cassandra, but she thought the corners of his lips twitched. Her skin pricked and she shivered.

'Are you cold? The heating in here doesn't seem to be on. It's only April, after all.'

'Yes, but it's been spring in Cornwall for a month. Officially. It was declared four weeks ago.'

It may have been spring, but there was no denying the cold. The truth was she'd turned off the radiators in all the private areas of the building months ago, trying to save on the fuel bill. 'Put on a vest, and another jumper' she'd advised anyone who complained about the cold and damp. As long as the guests were warm, everyone else could make do.

His eyebrows arched. 'Does spring come to Cornwall before anywhere else in the country?'

'Spring is declared in Cornwall when a champion magnolia in each of seven different Cornish gardens has fifty or more blooms fully open. That happened on the third of March.'

'Is the garden of the Hideaway one of the seven?'

'Well, no… People don't come here particularly to see the garden. It's grown a little wild.'

'Is "wild" a creative word for "neglected"? Like the building?'

'It's an old building. Ancient. There's always something needing to be fixed. It keeps our gardener, George, very busy…'

'Trying to stop the place from falling down and landing up on the beach.' He nodded towards the cove below. 'I had a conversation with George on my way in,' he continued. 'He said he'd like to grow enough vegetables and fruit in summer to supply the kitchen but much of his time is spent patching things up rather than on productive gardening.'

Cass wished George hadn't been quite so candid but what he'd said was true. And he would have been no match for the sort of intense questioning Matheo Chevalier would have directed at him. She'd defy anyone caught in the beam of those eyes not to tell all, immediately. She tried a different tack.

'George has been here a long time and he knows the building better than anyone now that my fa—' She breathed in and out again. 'Anyway, he knows every corner of the building, and all its weak spots. He can fix anything...'

He turned to face her fully, and his broad-shouldered frame blocked a significant amount of light from the window. 'This whole operation is a collection of weak spots held together by old habits and sentimentality, by the look of it,' he continued. 'George would be better employed doing what he says he does best and growing vegetables for the restaurant.' He pushed a hand through his hair. 'These days, everyone wants to know where their food was grown and how many air miles it took to get it onto their plates. Serving fresh, organic produce grown in the garden with zero carbon footprint would be a powerful marketing tool.'

'I know that.'

She'd thought about it, of course she had, but the constant round of necessary repairs had taken up most of George's time and there was no money to pay anyone else to do the work.

'You haven't acted on something you know

would obviously improve business,' Matheo said bluntly. 'Anyone who works for me gets fired for that sort of lapse.'

'Well, luckily I don't work for you,' she snapped.

'This hotel is dowdy, run-down, unexciting—the list is endless, and I don't expect to be impressed by the staff, either.'

Cass felt anger swelling in her chest. This man knew nothing of what it was like to hold your breath at the end of every month while you tried to balance the books, or how putting on an extra jumper in the winter might keep your body warmer but your fingers were still sometimes too cold to hit the right buttons on the keyboard. He'd had it easy all his life. All he'd had to do was follow in his father's arrogant footsteps.

'There are good people here. People who've been loyal and faithful to the hotel and to my family for years. They don't deserve to be discarded without a chance to prove themselves. Some of them know no other life, and—'

'What I need are people who know what they're doing and who have the initiative to get on with the job.'

'They all know what they're doing. Some of them have been here so long they could do their jobs blindfolded...'

Too late, Cass realised she'd played straight into his hands.

'Yes, that's what I thought. The first thing this

place needs is some new ideas and a fresh approach.'

Matheo Chevalier moved from the window and gestured to the desk. 'Shall we sit down, or would you prefer to stand by the window? It's slightly warmer there, in the sun.'

'The sun will be gone in a few minutes.'

'How do you know what the sun will do?'

If Cass hadn't known she couldn't possibly be right, she would have thought a hint of curiosity had crept into his voice.

'Because the wind has changed. Earlier today the sea was flat calm and a particular shade of blue, but now there are white caps on the swells and a weather front on the horizon. When it hits land, it'll rain and we won't see the sun again until tomorrow.'

And, she thought, I'll have to sleep on the sofa in the staff sitting room again. Her little attic room had a leak in the roof which even George had been unable to mend, and the rain would drip relentlessly onto her narrow childhood bed.

He looked out at the sea, his gaze narrowed. 'I suppose if you've spent your entire life in a place you get to be able to predict the weather. I've never had that…' He stopped and Cass wondered if his frown was one of regret or simply of incomprehension.

He pulled up a second chair and Cassandra watched as he removed his jacket and slung it over the back of what had been her chair until he'd decided to use it. He inserted a forefinger into the knot of his tie, pulling it loose and undoing the top button of his shirt, exposing the smooth golden skin in the hollow where his neck joined his shoulder, and the protuberance of his collar bone.

Then he removed a pair of heavy gold cufflinks and rolled up his sleeves. He crossed his arms, resting his muscled forearms on the desk.

'Mademoiselle Greenwood? Will you sit down?' A corner of his mouth lifted as he regarded her. 'There are a few things I'd like to discuss with you before finalising my bid.' He glanced towards the door. 'Will the coffee arrive soon, do you think?'

Cass lowered herself onto the edge of the chair beside him.

'I usually go and get what I need. So shall I…?'

She began to rise again but he shook his head, just firmly enough to show who was in charge.

He looked up as a soft tap sounded at the door.

'Ah. And here it is.'

Cass sat down again. How did he do that? Even Tess had listened to him.

'Thank you, Tess. The coffee smells excellent. Could you put it on the desk, please?'

Tess carried a tray across the room, her bottom lip caught in her teeth. She placed it on the desk and backed away.

'Um… I brought sandwiches. It's almost lunchtime and I know Cass hasn't had br—'

Cass shot Tess a look and she closed her mouth.

'Thank you. And please will you inform the restaurant I'll be dining there tonight, and I hope Mademoiselle Greenwood will join me?'

'Oh, but Cass and I go to our yoga class on Mondays. Cass, aren't you…?'

'That'll be all, Tess, thank you,' he said.

'Yes, Mr Chevalier, of course.' Tess almost ran from the room.

Dinner with him in the restaurant was quite possibly the worst idea Cass had ever heard. And anyway, she was busy. The yoga class shone like a beacon of hope at the end of what was becoming a difficult day.

'Thank you, Mr Chevalier, but I won't be able to join you for dinner. I'm busy this evening.'

'Could you skip yoga tonight?'

'But may I suggest you make a reservation at a restaurant in town instead?' she carried on, ignoring him. 'I don't think the Hideaway serves the sort of food people…um…like you prefer to eat.'

The crease between his brows deepened.

'What sort of food do "people like me" prefer?'

Cass felt herself flushing. She had the feeling he was hiding amusement behind that frown.

'I think you know what I mean. Our menu consists of plain, old-fashioned dishes of the meat and two veg variety. It's what our loyal guests expect.

People who've been coming here year after year don't like change.'

'Ah. And can I expect jelly and custard for pudding?'

'It might be spotted dick this evening.'

Two could play at this game.

'Good,' he countered smoothly. 'It'll be like being back at my English boarding school.' His mouth curved and she noticed the hint of a dimple in his cheek. 'It'll remind me how happy I was to be expelled. But I presume your…yoga class… won't last all evening?'

His tone rated yoga somewhere on a level with English boarding schools. Cass thought if she had to dine with him, she might stab him with a steak knife.

'Can you talk me through some figures?' He pulled a slim laptop from the case on the desk and flipped it open. 'I'm hoping you'll be able to clarify a couple of things. Then they might make less depressing reading than the accounts for the last financial year your lawyer provided.'

That, thought Cass, was highly unlikely.

CHAPTER TWO

QUITE QUICKLY, he found the figures could depress him deeply. For the first time, Matheo Chevalier questioned his interest in this failing hotel. What was driving his desire for it? Was his need for revenge really worth it? Instead of feeling excited by the prospect of acquiring what generations of his family had craved, he felt weighed down by the possibility.

He searched in vain for a single positive thing to focus on. What the hell had Joe Greenwood been thinking of over the past fourteen years? Whatever it was, it had had nothing to do with running a profitable hotel and everything to do with preserving some sort of time capsule. Then he pushed himself away from the desk, allowed himself to be irritated by the squeaking wheel on the elderly chair, and swivelled towards Cassandra. She sat, chin sunk into her palm, staring out at the teeming rain. Her gaze was unfocused, and he wondered what her life had been like, living with a father who had evidently paid no attention to the world around him, and probably not to his daughter either, at a time when she would have desperately needed security and comfort.

She'd lost her mother and then her father and she was about to lose her home. None of it made him feel good. He considered what it must be like to feel the loss of family so deeply and realised he had no idea. His memories of his mother consisted of acute sadness and then lonely isolation in his English boarding school. He tried to take a mental step back, to make this less personal, but for some reason totally unfamiliar to him it was difficult. The room was colder than ever and he allowed himself to blame that for his feeling of uncertainty and irritation.

'Does that fireplace work?' He looked at the impressive carved chimney breast then frowned at the smoke-black stain on the wall above it. 'If it does, why don't we light a fire?'

Cass got to her feet and walked over to the Victorian iron radiator under the window. Bending down, she did something to the valve and a loud gurgling sound rumbled from the pipes.

'Since I will shortly no longer have responsibility for the heating bills, I've turned it onto maximum. We'll be warm as toast in a few minutes.'

He had trouble believing what he was hearing. 'Are all the radiators in the hotel turned off?'

Cass shook her head. 'Only the ones in the private areas. We've always made sure our guests are warm and dry. But the cost of heating increases constantly, and the system is antiquated. I knew we wouldn't be able to afford the oil for much longer.'

'Is that "we" as in you and your father?'

She laughed. 'No. My father had all the radiators on and the heating going full blast for most of the year. Being cold or damp just increased his misery, and Cornwall can be both of those, even in summer.'

'Was it only after he died that you began to put cost-saving measures into place?'

'It was only after he died that I had anything at all to do with running the hotel.'

Matheo tried to hide his surprise. He'd assumed she'd always been here, a part of this ramshackle arrangement of rooms that called itself a hotel. It was worse than he'd thought possible.

'What were you doing before?'

'I was working. In London.'

He found he wanted to know exactly what it was she'd been doing in London. What had become of the wild teenager he remembered? The one with the long, long dark hair and deep blue eyes, running away down the beach when he had attempted to talk to her. He recalled how, after their first, brief encounter, she had scrambled over the rocks and vanished.

It was as if when the next wave came in and washed her footprints from the sand it had washed her away too. That wayward teenager in the gypsy skirt and seashell necklace had been erased. In her place stood this serious, defensive young woman, with her wild hair severely tamed. And an air of only just hanging on to her emotions.

An utterly foreign sensation unfurled somewhere behind his breastbone. It took him a moment to identify it as regret. She was hurting and he and his family were partly to blame. He wished he could change that.

Matheo massaged the base of his skull. He blinked, trying to blot out the thought, but instead found himself focusing on the disturbing image that had burned itself onto his retinas—the image of Cassandra's endless legs, in faded blue jeans, as she had bent over the valve of the radiator. He groaned inwardly. This was not the time or the place to entertain regrets or to lust after a pair of legs, but the punch of desire which the sight of them had dealt to his stomach was real. He needed to get out of here and go for a five-mile run to kill these inappropriate and massively misplaced thoughts.

He tried to focus on all the negatives he'd uncovered in the past couple of hours, but there were too many. At least the attempt took his mind off the slim woman who stood looking out of the window, ignoring him.

'What are you thinking about?' he asked, his curiosity surprising him.

'I'm thinking,' she replied calmly, leaning against the radiator, 'that you're right.'

'What about?' He frowned, trying to second-guess her. 'The staff?'

She lifted her chin and shook her head. 'No. I was thinking that my position *is* impossibly weak. I'll be pressured into accepting the highest offer, even if it's not what I want to do. The idea of selling to you is almost unbearable, but if you—'

Matheo, against his expectations, had to admit to being intrigued. An inner strength seemed to enable Cassandra to hold herself together. And what other woman he'd ever met could predict the weather by looking at the sky or know that the arrival of spring depended on the whim of a flowering tree and not on the solid evidence of the calendar?

'I'll offer enough to enable you to clear your debts,' he interrupted. 'That way you can walk away…'

'But that's just it,' she said, softly. 'I don't want to walk away. I want to do my best to ensure that the members of staff—at least those who want to stay—are given a chance.'

He turned to face her fully. The quick rise and fall of her chest under her jumper belied her steady voice.

'I'll agree to consider any offer you make for the Hideaway if you'll agree to certain things. Two things, actually.'

'What two things?'

'Firstly, that you'll give the staff members the opportunity to prove themselves. They don't deserve to be thrown out without a chance.'

'And the second?' He noticed the beat of the pulse at her throat quicken.

'That you allow me to have a say in the renovations.'

He propped his chin on a fist and watched her. Her expression was impassive, but he'd already noticed the physical signs of stress.

'I don't think either of those things are going to happen, Miss Greenwood.'

'Then I don't think I'm going to sell to you, Mr Chevalier.' Defiance flashed in her eyes.

'You need my money, and I don't need you or your staff, so you don't have any bargaining power. A deal must be mutually beneficial to both parties. That's how it works.'

'I can refuse to sell to you.'

'You can, but I don't think you will. Think of the alternative. The burden of debt, the threat of bankruptcy. And your lawyers will put you under pressure.'

'You're assuming the employees are no good.'

'There's no room in business for sentiment. Every single member of staff, from the doorman to the manager, needs to have pride in their position and be prepared to give one hundred and ten per cent all the time.'

'You're jumping to negative conclusions when you know nothing about them.'

'Maybe, but I think I'm justified. It doesn't look as if anything has changed here for fifty years, from the décor to the housekeeper, and probably the mattresses.'

'As I said, our loyal guests don't appreciate change.'

'And the average age of your typical loyal guest is?'

She hesitated. 'I don't know. Most of them are elderly.'

'You *should* know. What's going to happen when they're unable to holiday here any longer? You need to attract a younger, hipper, *wealthier* guest, and to do that a lot is going to have to change.'

There was a pause, and when she answered defeat coloured her voice.

'Yes, I've realised that.'

'And why are you worried about the staff when you won't be here anylonger?'

He wished he could take those words back. *Of course* she worried about the staff. He was fast learning she was that kind of person, and it made this whole process of acquisition difficult when it had never been difficult before.

She stared at him. ‘Forgive me for saying so, Mr Chevalier, but that is a silly question. I *care* about them, that’s why, but perhaps you don’t know what it’s like to feel personally responsible for other people’s livelihoods and wellbeing. Mrs Brown, the housekeeper, cared for my mother when she was ill. George searched for me when I ran away, after she died. The chef has baked me a birthday cake every year I’ve been here, and he’s done the same for countless others.’

She stopped, and he saw she was breathing fast. There was a flush on her cheeks and her eyes were bright with what looked suspiciously like tears.

‘Do you need any more reasons?’ she finished.

‘Are there any? And I’m sorry if I’ve upset you.’ He felt appalled at the raw emotion in her expression and her voice, and desperate to stop it. Losing control of a situation, especially one of his own making, was a new experience for him and one which he disliked. He wondered how it had happened after a few short hours in Cassandra’s company.

She brushed the edge of a finger under her eyes.

‘It’s too late for tears. I just wish you wouldn’t judge people without any evidence. Money may fix many things, but it can’t mend relationships or buy simple human kindness. Perhaps one day you’ll discover that for yourself.’

Matheo stood up, trying to regain control. How had this happened? What should have been a day spent familiarising himself with the business so he could fine-tune his bid had turned into an emotional roller-coaster ride. He'd always hated roller coasters. The sense of being out of control, of not knowing what would hit you next, was unbearable. His stomach swooped and with a jolt of alarm he realised that Cassandra Greenwood, whose legs had already proved to be dangerously distracting, was altogether much too beautiful. Her violet eyes shimmered like amethysts in her pale face. Her dark hair, so severely styled, had rebelled, and a few wayward tendrils had worked their way out of the knot to curl against the creamy skin of her neck.

He pressed his palms onto the desktop and hauled his attention back to the conversation they'd been having.

'I asked, Mademoiselle Greenwood,' he said, the effort it took making his voice tight, 'if there were any more reasons why you think the members of your team should be kept on. *Are* there?'

He watched her struggle to keep calm. Her fingers gripped the iron radiator on either side of her hips, and her chest rose and fell erratically, but she looked at him without flinching, her violet gaze direct and challenging.

'I've…given them the impression that they may have a few months' trial under the new ownership.' She pushed a lock of hair off her face with a hand which trembled slightly. 'But I should have realised that was just a dream born of desperation. Anyway, by now Tess will have told them—*all* of them—who you are, and although they will never believe I'd sell to you they'll know their jobs are lost if I do.' She pressed her hands together. 'The Chevalier name is mud at this hotel.'

She glanced out of the window, and he followed her gaze, but there was nothing to see but grey clouds scudding over a grey sea, and rain coming down in sheets. He was no longer cold, though he wasn't sure if his warmth was as a result of the radiator, which had creaked into life, or of the charged atmosphere in the room.

'I've told them any new owner will hopefully put money into the hotel, to fix all the things that need fixing, get new equipment for the kitchen, rebuild the quay and restore the boat so we can offer sailing trips again… The list of what we haven't been able to afford is endless.'

Matheo ground the heels of his hands into his eye sockets and rubbed. Then he dropped his hands and walked across the room towards her. She straightened.

'I don't think you've been thinking logically.'

'I was thinking that I could soften the blow if I could tell them they still had a chance of keeping their jobs. I thought I might be able to influence any new owner's plans for the building, so that some of its character could be preserved.' She lifted her shoulders in a gesture of resignation.

'If you and your father had run the place properly you wouldn't be in this position now. If I make the offer I've mentioned it will be in excess of the value of what is barely a going concern, but if I buy it, by the end of the year the Hideaway will be one of the most desirable boutique hotels in the country. I cannot run it as a charity for the sake of the workforce.'

'My father believed the people were as important—no, more important—than the profit. He was caring and humane and money meant nothing to him.'

'Unfortunately, money becomes very important when you don't have enough of it. If you'd paid more attention to the business before your father died you might have realised just what sort of state his affairs were in. What were you doing in London? You should have been here.' The look she sent him made him feel suddenly a little unsure of his ground. 'I mean, then perhaps you'd have realised what was happening.'

'I was building the company in which I'm a partner.' She paused and he tried to hide his surprise, recalibrate his opinion of her. 'But,' she continued, 'if the Hideaway is such a disaster, I suggest you reconsider. Or is the opportunity to get hold of it just too tempting to resist? Is revenge really that sweet?'

'It has nothing at all to do with the revenge you imply and everything to do with spotting a business that can be turned around and made profitable,' he retorted, trying to regain the advantage. Cassandra, in her navy fisherman's jumper and worn denims, looked nothing like a businesswoman. He couldn't even hazard a guess at what sort of company she was building. 'It can be done with any business. I happen to do it with property, mainly hotels.'

'Credit me with a little more intelligence and insight than that. I clearly remember your father doing his utmost to buy the Hideaway from my father fourteen years ago, when he thought he'd caught him at a low ebb. What sort of person descends on a man broken by grief, and tries to force him to sell his home and livelihood?'

'If your father had sold then…'

'That's not the point.' She lifted her chin. 'The sort of man who would do that is the sort who was hell-bent on revenge, because his family had never been able to accept that the hotel belonged to *us*. My father denied yours that triumph, and I'd love to deny it to you.' She pushed her hands into her pockets, and he thought they were shaking.

He moved away from her and returned to stand behind the desk. 'Revenge would, indeed, be sweet, but not necessarily for the reasons you think.'

'I don't know what that means. Now, if you'll excuse me, I need to speak to the staff.'

Cassandra turned and walked towards the door, her back ramrod straight and her head high. It was all Matheo could do to stop himself from reaching out a restraining hand to stop her. She might look vulnerable in unguarded moments, but she had an enviable core of steel, which would take her a long way if she chose to head in the right direction. She was the sort of person he liked to hire—personable, approachable, and with a titanium-strength self-belief. He dismissed the thought, only for it to be replaced by the far more disturbing one of how it would feel to hold that delicate face between his hands and… He wouldn't begin to go there. He couldn't, not now. He was exhausted, not thinking straight. When last had he had a long enough night's sleep? He didn't know. He'd have to get out for some fresh air. But then he thought of something he wanted to know.

'Mademoiselle Greenwood?'

She stopped in the doorway, keeping her back to him.

'What is your company?'

She turned, her narrow shoulders lifted.

'It's called FuturePlan. We remodel and re-purpose hotels and buildings like this one.' She shrugged. 'Which is why I suggested I could be involved in this project. We're a small company, so our overheads are lower, which would keep the cost down…'

He held up a hand.

'Hang on. Let me get this right.' He folded his arms across his chest. 'You're suggesting that I employ you to work on the renovation of this hotel? To keep costs down?' He shook his head. 'Are you familiar with any of the Chevalier work?'

Cassandra took two steps back into the room.

'Of course I am. Your hotels are famous. They're huge and modern; stunning pieces of architecture and insane levels of luxury. But you haven't done anything like this before, have you? The Hideaway is unique and iconic in its own way, and I know it better than anyone. We have ideas, Nick and I—good ideas—about how it could be.'

'Nick?'

'He's my partner in FuturePlan. The chief architect. I head up the interior-design team.'

'And you have ideas which haven't been put into practice?'

'No, they haven't,' she answered, shaking her head. 'There's been no money. And anyway, my father refused…' Her eyes dropped to the floor. 'My father didn't want anything to change.' She took a deep breath, and her eyes met his again. 'My idea was that we could do the remodelling, using my knowledge of the building and the local area, if the new owners would give the staff the chance to prove themselves.' She turned and walked back to the door.

This time Matheo did not try to stop her. The room felt darker after she'd left. He checked the light bulbs in the ancient fittings before deciding it was the leaden clouds outside that had stolen the light.

He still needed to resolve some discrepancies in the figures with her, but if necessary he'd employ his forensic accountant to unravel the mystery. But he needed to move quickly. He thought it very likely that she'd sell to anyone but him if she could.

If asked to guess what Cassandra Greenwood did for a living, he would never have got it right. He tried to avoid making assumptions in life—they could so often trip you up—but he realised he'd come to the possible purchase of the Hideaway with very little idea of what actually lay behind its ancient stone walls. Cassandra's offer was bold, and he admired that, but he had no intention of agreeing to it. Why would he risk employing a small, unknown company when he could choose whoever he wanted to do the work?

He returned to the window and took in the vista. A grey sea heaved under an angry grey sky and grey rain blurred the boundary between them. There was no room in his life for doubts or regrets, which was fortunate, he thought, as otherwise he'd be entertaining a whole room full of them right now. But he wasn't letting them in. There was no reason why this hotel couldn't become a great success story, just like his others. Okay, it was different from the sort of project he normally took on but that didn't mean it would be more difficult. The lawyers working on behalf of Cassandra Greenwood would talk her round, make her see financial sense, and she'd accept his offer.

He knew that the regret which nagged at him had nothing at all to do with buying the hotel and everything to do with the person from whom he planned to buy it. He usually dealt with faceless names on a contract. But he'd been tricked by his memories into coming here in person and it had been a huge mistake. The dark-haired girl with the amethyst eyes had danced on the edge of his consciousness for fourteen years and the temptation to discover what had happened to her had overridden his legendary cool reason and calculated good sense.

He sat down in the squeaky chair and returned his attention to the computer screen. He'd go through the figures one more time, but he knew there was something wrong. He'd picked it up straight away, but he just couldn't work out how it was happening.

He stretched his arms and folded them behind his head and found his eyes straying to the window again. If this was his office, the first thing he'd do was turn the desk around so that his back was to the view and he could see exactly who was coming through the door. The whole layout of the room, he realised, was a microcosm of the rest of the place. It was casual to the point of being chaotic. The sagging sofa looked suspiciously as if a large dog had been sleeping on it for years and the threadbare Persian rug needed a good shake-out—or possibly throw-out. There was a row of shells on the window ledge and a row of cards on the dusty bookshelf.

Curious, he went over and peered at them. They were thank-you cards, a few dating back years, some with the same scrawled signatures at the end of effusive messages of gratitude for days and weeks spent at the Hideaway. Cassandra had said they had loyal guests who returned time and time again, and here was the proof.

He shut down the computer, dropped his phone into his trouser pocket and picked up his jacket. He needed to get out of here.

Cass didn't want to see anyone and the chances were good that she wouldn't. Their few guests would be dozing in the sitting room, replete with their afternoon cream tea, and the kitchen staff would be preparing dinner. There ought to be someone at the reception desk, but with luck...

She started up the stairs and met Tess coming down. She was in her purple leggings and pink top.

'Cass! I've been waiting for you. Aren't we going to yoga?'

'Oh, Tess, I don't think I'm in the right frame of mind for yoga now.'

'He made you cry! Oh, Cass, I hate him. I want to slap him. I—'

'No! I haven't been crying.'

Cass put a hand to her face and found it was wet with tears.

'Well, if I have it's because I'm so frustrated.' She sniffed. 'He…he just wouldn't listen to me.'

Tess nodded vigorously. 'He's *way* too sure of himself. And *way* too smooth to be cool.' Then her expression changed, her eyes taking on a far-away look. 'But he was nice about the coffee. And his voice…' She put a hand on Cass's arm. 'I'm sorry, Cass. But you won't sell the Hideaway to him, will you?'

Cass scrubbed a hand over her face, knowing she'd be smudging her make-up. This morning, when she'd put it on, felt like a lifetime away. She dropped her eyes and studied her feet. 'I'm so sorry about what's happened, Tess. This is all exactly what my dad would not have wanted, but I just don't know. And I'm tired of the struggle.' She shook her head. 'He says he'll pay enough to clear all the debts, and that's very tempting, but then I think of my dad and I'm determined I'll never sell to a Chevalier…'

Tess squeezed her shoulder. 'Maybe yoga is just what you need, Cass. Space to recharge and reset?'

'Space to cry, and I can't afford that. You go. Maybe I'll see you later.'

She pushed past Tess and took the stairs to the attic two at a time.

CHAPTER THREE

MATHEO'S FEET POUNDED the beach, his arms and legs pumping. The sand was a little soft for running, but that was good. He needed a tough workout, requiring mental and physical effort, if there was any hope of clearing his head. His plans for the Hideaway had been sharp and clear-sighted, but Cassandra's suggestion of a deal had blurred them, casting doubt on his usually straightforward thinking. He was properly warm, for what felt like the first time in hours, but the sweat trickling off him was immediately sluiced away by the driving rain. His chest heaved as he sucked in deep, fast breaths but he pushed himself harder.

The waves of the full tide heaved themselves out of the sea and crashed against the foot of the rough cliffs at the end of the beach and he stopped, frustration bubbling through him. His planned route along the water's edge was blocked. He could turn back and retrace his steps or attempt the run up the overgrown path which snaked through the tumbled rocks towards the clifftop.

But as his eyes followed the line of the track upwards, he froze. A figure stood silhouetted against the racing grey clouds, perilously close to the edge. Dark hair streamed behind her in the wind, and as he watched she turned abruptly and disappeared.

He launched himself into a sprint towards the foot of the cliff.

The climb was challenging and by the time he scrambled onto the top, grabbing at tussocks of wet grass to heave himself up, it felt as if his lungs were on fire. He got to his feet, vaulted over a low gate and continued, without breaking his stride, along the side of a stone church.

His pace picked up again on the level ground and he turned the corner of the building at full speed. Then he slithered to an abrupt stop as he saw Cassandra coming towards him.

'Mademoiselle Greenwood.' His chest heaved as he filled his burning lungs with the cool, damp air. 'Are you alright?'

'Were you following me?' she asked, stopping and wiping the rain off her face with a sleeve.

'No. I was out for a run.' He glanced backwards, the way he'd come. 'On the beach, and I saw you…'

His breath began to steady and he shook his hair out of his eyes and studied her. It was impossible to tell whether her face was wet with tears or rain.

He looked away, over her head, and realised she'd been standing in a small graveyard. The ground sloped away towards the cliff edge but from the beach it had looked as if she'd been about to launch herself over the edge.

His knee-jerk reaction had almost made him look like an idiot. He never acted on impulse. He'd learned that lesson long ago, watching his father's calculated actions. He weighed up every situation, every deal, with the utmost care, the coolest head, before making a considered response.

'You startled me. Hardly anyone else ever comes here.'

'I'm…sorry.' The apology sounded like a foreign word to him. 'I…thought maybe you needed help. The wind is fierce. It's slippery underfoot…'

'Thank you.' She nodded. 'But I'm fine.'

'I thought you'd be talking to the staff.'

She glanced behind her, towards the gravestones. 'I had to do this first. It'll be dark by the time I've finished the staff meetings.'

She stepped around him and he turned to watch her as she walked away.

She clicked the gate closed behind her, and then broke into a jog.

When she'd been swallowed up in the gloom Matheo turned and walked into the teeth of the wind, which roared off the sea and over the cliff-top, flattening the grass and the clumps of daffodils which grew among the headstones.

He soon found her parents' names and stood looking down at the neatly tended mounds. He tried to put himself in Cassandra's shoes, wondering how she felt, but it was impossible. The desperately sad look he'd seen in her sparkling eyes was beyond his experience.

Then he swept his dripping hair out of his eyes and turned back, viciously crushing the stirring of something—pity?—which threatened to undermine his resolution. If he allowed pity to inform his decisions he'd be running a charity, not a mega-billions company.

The descent of the cliff path was even more difficult than the ascent had been, but he tackled it at full speed, despite the dangers posed by the slippery surface and loose pebbles. He wasn't finished yet—he still had more energy to expend today than most people had in a week. Besides, he needed to snuff out a treacherous little glow that threatened to ignite in his belly.

Cass didn't slow to a walk until she was sure she'd put a good distance between herself and Matheo Chevalier. What had that been about? Why would Matheo Chevalier, the latest in a long line of Chevaliers to want to crush her family, rush to her aid? They'd shown nothing but contempt and disdain for the Greenwoods for generations and she couldn't believe Matheo was any different. Not if he was his father's son.

Her mind flashed back to earlier in the day when she'd tumbled into his arms at the foot of the ladder. What strange power did he wield over her senses that he could make her want to let him protect her? The feeling went against all the principles by which she lived her independent life.

Was it simply because it was so long since she'd had any physical contact with a man? She tried not to think about Jason. She felt too vulnerable and stressed to allow those memories any breathing space, but as usual that meant they were able to slide in and grab her attention. They'd met when she'd started her first job as an assistant in the interiors department of a large company. She'd been flattered that a member of the accounts department had noticed her and had taken the trouble to lavish care and attention on her. With hindsight she realised she'd been an easy target. He'd recognised her vulnerability, but he hadn't been interested in discovering its roots. He'd exploited it to indulge his need to dominate and control. At the time it had been a relief to allow someone else to look after her, after the years of caring for her mother in her illness and then her father in his depression. But then, bit by bit, he'd become possessive, demanding to know where she was at all times, and beginning to dictate all kinds of limitations on her life. He'd wanted her to move in with him and she'd been afraid of his fury when she'd refused.

When she discovered he'd put a tracker on her phone she'd known she had to end it.

It had been tough. It would have been so much easier just to give in to his demands. At first she'd missed the security the relationship had given her, after the chaotic life she'd been forced to live after her mother's death, but she'd not been prepared to pay the price he seemed to feel she owed him for it. She'd called on the strength she'd gained through the difficult years and used every ounce of it. Now she felt confident she'd never again put herself at the mercy of anyone else, because she'd grown strong enough to lead the life she wanted on her own terms. She just wasn't always strong enough to block the memories of how he'd treated her.

She'd met Nick and together they'd formed FuturePlan. A few years later, with a combination of a lot of talent and a little luck, they'd completed three small but prestigious projects and had just signed a deal which, if successful, would raise their profile massively.

She'd travelled extensively in search of the best of everything for the striking interiors she designed. Her professional self-confidence in her taste, her instinctive eye for the unusual had strengthened with each challenge, but on a personal level the experience with Jason had left her anxious and wary, with issues involving trust and honesty.

Her father had been destroyed by the loss of his soulmate. She herself had almost been crushed by a man who said he loved her but only if she stuck to the rules he made.

Love, she'd decided, was a brutal, dangerous game.

And then her father had died.

Matheo Chevalier was a businessman, just like his father, with a ruthless approach and a lack of sensitivity to the needs of others which would make Genghis Khan look like a philanthropist. She needed to remember *that*.

Her father had despised his father, her grandfather his grandfather. And she should despise them all.

If she'd been tired before, Cassandra reflected, she was beyond exhaustion by ten o'clock. The emotional strain of the day was catching up with her, fast. She had to stop before she collapsed, and, feeling as she did, that was a scarily real possibility.

The meetings with the staff had been horrible, even though most of them had suspected what was coming. The ancient enmity between the Chevalier and Greenwood clans was well-known, and as soon as Tess, round-eyed and bursting with an air of conspiracy, had announced the name of the latest man bidding to be the new owner, any hopes of a reprieve had been dashed.

The kitchen was dark and eerily quiet, but through the fog of fatigue she managed to find one of the standby ready meals she kept in the freezer. She slammed the door of the elderly microwave and cranked the dial. It whirred, clicked and pinged. Then she carried the container to the staff sitting room, curled up on the sofa and began to eat, staring out at the darkness and listening to the steady beat of the rain. She felt unable to comprehend how this could be her last night under the roof of the creaking old building that had been home for her entire life.

Matheo had stared at the columns of figures on the screen until his eyes ached. His frustration was in danger of tipping over into anger. When had he ever not understood a spreadsheet? Never, was the answer. Never, until now. The figures simply didn't work.

He stood up and massaged his temples with his fingertips. He wished he were on St Celeste, where he controlled everything that happened, from one warm day to the next.

His discreet, quiet staff on the Mediterranean island were the few people he trusted implicitly these days. The sense of peace and security that enveloped him each time he returned was addictive and he'd become increasingly reluctant to leave. Most of his business could be conducted remotely and he bitterly regretted ignoring his better judgement and coming to see the Hideaway for himself. It had been unnecessary and he was paying the price.

Emotion had intruded on what should have been a straightforward business deal. The two did not mix and he should have known to stay away. Perhaps he should reconsider, let the past go and get on with his life. But he recognised that his pride was a huge stumbling block.

He ran a hand over his jaw, rough at this late hour. The kitchen would be closed, but perhaps he'd be able to find some coffee somewhere. He regretted leaving the restaurant before the grim-faced waiter had brought him a pot earlier, but he couldn't wait to get away. The meal had been mediocre, the atmosphere depressing, with just two other tables occupied by couples he could only assume had been coming here so long they were practically a part of the furnishings.

And the furnishings were another thing. Dusty, faded, and so dated someone kinder might have dubbed them 'vintage'.

The entire hotel appeared to be deserted, the quiet broken only by the soft creaks of the ancient inn as it settled for the night. In the distance he could hear the thunder of the surf on the shore and the rain still rattled in fierce gusts against the mullioned windows. Remembering the layout from the plans of the building he'd studied, he made his way towards the kitchen. Dim wall lamps provided low-level lighting in the passages, but the public rooms were in darkness. Then he spotted a faint bar of light glowing beneath a door.

Cassandra Greenwood slept, curled up, on a sofa under the window. Her cheek rested on one hand while the fingers of the other held a fork, which in turn lay in the plastic tray of some sort of half-eaten meal. Her dark hair rippled in glossy waves over the cushions.

Matheo stopped, his breath catching in his chest. An inner voice exhorted him not to break the spell. He thought he'd never seen anyone look more beautiful, or more tired, even in sleep, in his life. She still wore the jeans and cable-knit sweater in which he'd seen her last, and he frowned. The clothes must be damp and cold, even though she'd worn a rain jacket. With infinite care, he stepped forward, picked up a plaid rug which was draped over the back of the sofa, and dropped it over her.

She shot upright, sending the remains of the food flying onto the floor and the fork clattering into a corner.

'Mademoiselle Greenwood, what are you doing here? Haven't you got a bed to sleep in?' He spoke quietly, as if still afraid to wake her.

'That's the second time today you've scared me.' She shook her head and pushed her fingers through her hair. 'And no… I mean…yes, but it's wet.'

'I didn't mean… *Wet?* Why is it wet?'

'There's a leak in the roof above it.'

'Well, why haven't you had it fixed? What about George? Why hasn't he done it?'

'It only leaks when the wind blows in a certain direction.' She glanced towards the window. 'The rain gets in under the lead. And George has tried but he's always too busy mending the bits that matter.'

'And you having no bed to sleep in doesn't matter?'

'No, not really. This may be an old sofa but it's comfortable.' She gathered her hair behind her head and twisted it in her hands, then she let it fall and stretched up her arms, before folding them across her chest.

'I apologise for startling you.' He may have startled her twice, but he had apologised twice, too. This was unfamiliar territory. 'I was hoping to find some coffee.' He shrugged. 'I don't suppose there is a hope in hell of anyone answering if I ring the bell at the front desk?'

'Absolutely no hope at all.' Her smile was slight, but even so a dimple faintly indented her cheek. 'You're getting the hang of things. Everyone either went home or went to bed hours ago.

If you want coffee, you'll have to make it yourself.' She leaned back against the sofa cushions, wriggling her shoulders. 'There's a tin in that cupboard.'

'And I suppose it'll be instant, yes?'

A slight twitch at the corner of her mouth made him feel she found the situation amusing. Then she nodded, once.

Matheo frowned. 'The coffee Tess provided was very good. It wasn't instant.' He wondered whether to give up and return to the infuriating spreadsheet. But giving up wasn't his style. He looked around and saw a kettle, a sink and a fridge. 'Would you like a cup, always assuming I can find it?'

'There are camomile teabags in the cupboard. I'll have a mug of that, thanks.' She stifled a yawn. 'Then I might have a chance of getting back to sleep before I have to wake up again.'

Matheo opened the cupboard above the kettle. A shiny glass and chrome cafetière stood on the shelf, alongside a tin of instant coffee and a motley collection of mugs. Several of the mugs had slogans on them—*Drama Queen*, said one, and *Don't Tell Me to Keep Calm* another. *I'd Rather be Somewhere Else*, stated a third. He hesitated, wondering about what sort of message he wanted to send, and then he grabbed the nearest two and placed them rather too firmly on the work surface.

When had he ever considered what message

a mug might send? When had he ever *cared*? Something about Cassandra's presence was messing with his mind and playing games with his body, sending inappropriate and frankly unacceptable messages on route marches all over it.

In the fridge he found a packet of French coffee, next to the milk.

Her voice came from behind him and he could hear the smile in it.

'Sorry. Your expectations were obviously so low it felt like a pity to disappoint you. I'd still like the camomile, though.'

Matheo kept his back to her and took a moment to absorb the fact that she was laughing at him. It wasn't something he tolerated and it hadn't happened for a very long time. He waited to feel annoyed. But then he realised that instead of the anger he should have felt, the idea of her smiling, at anything, made everything feel a little better.

He made the coffee and tea and carried the mugs over to the sofa. Cassandra sat cross-legged on the cushions. She took the mug of tea in both hands and wrapped her fingers around its warmth, inhaling the sweet aroma.

Matheo continued to stand.

'Sit down, if you like.' She waved her mug at a pair of faded armchairs.

He drew in a deep, unsteady breath and then sipped from the mug. *I'd Rather be Somewhere Else*, it announced to him. Too right. *Anywhere* else, to be precise. He saw that Cass's mug said *Angel*, with an irritating little halo above the 'A'. Perhaps it said *Devil* on the other side.

He was pleased she hadn't suggested he share the sofa with her. She intrigued him and her nearness made his blood pound in his veins and his thought processes feel alien, his reactions unpredictable.

He needed to sort out this confusion. He needed to get himself under control.

He sat down on one of the chairs, leaning forward and propping his elbows on his knees. 'I think I'll have to get my forensic accountant to solve the financial complications I've come across. But if you don't mind company, I'll see if you can shed any light on the problem first.'

Cass sipped from her mug, staring down at the floor. He followed her gaze and saw the spilled food she'd knocked from the sofa.

'I didn't realise you were getting a takeaway.'

'It was a ready meal from the freezer.'

'Why didn't you change? You shouldn't sleep in damp clothes.'

Matheo had returned from his run and taken a hot shower. At least there had been hot water and the shower, once it had got going, had worked.

'Most of my things are packed, ready to leave. I hadn't planned to go out and get soaked.'

She put her mug on the floor and stretched again and Matheo dragged his eyes away from the strip of ivory skin at her midriff, and the tantalising glimpse of the small indentation of her navel.

'You'd been to visit your parents' graves.'

'Yes.'

'I'm sorry.'

Her eyelids flew up and her gaze was startled, surprise briefly masking pain.

'That's what I said to them, with good reason. But why are *you* sorry? You think you're about to achieve what generations of your family have failed at. You should be…expectantly triumphant.'

Matheo closed his eyes and pinched the bridge of his nose, wondering how to express compassion. When he opened them again, he saw she was watching him, waiting for his answer.

He nodded. 'Yes, but I'm sorry…' He searched for the words. 'I'm sorry for your pain. For your loss. Of everything.' He wasn't at all sure where the sentiments had come from but expressing them made him feel a little less conflicted. 'And I'm sorry your relatives left you with this mess. If your father had paid any attention at all to running this hotel properly, you and I wouldn't be having this conversation.'

'I'm not at all sure about that. Your family has been hell-bent on getting the Hideaway back ever since your great-grandfather lost it to mine.' She tipped her head up to study the ceiling and later

Matheo thought that was the moment when the fight went out of her. He felt a sense of unreasonable panic, anxious to see her spirit return, to spar with him. He felt as if he'd crushed something beautiful and delicate and couldn't see any way to repair it.

'We were fine,' she continued, her voice quiet, 'until my mother died, but my dad just let things slide after that. He'd mortgaged the place to pay for her treatment and there was never going to be any way he could pay that back.' She shrugged. 'He'd started gambling to try and make the money we needed. I didn't know anything about that until after he died…'

Like his grandfather, he thought, but he clamped his mouth shut before the hurtful words could escape.

'Perhaps,' he said carefully, instead, 'gambling was a family weakness?'

He saw her fingers tighten around the angel-devil mug, the fine bones of her knuckles gleaming beneath the skin. 'My great-grandfather won the Hideaway from yours in a perfectly fair game of cards. That your ancestor was so arrogant and reckless with his property was something I've never understood.'

'My father says the game wasn't fair.'

'From my sixteen-year-old point of view, your father seemed arrogant. Perhaps that's your family weakness?'

'You're entitled to your opinion, obviously. It doesn't change the fact that your father—'

'Please stop talking about my father.' Her voice was brittle with strain. 'He didn't plan to die and leave me with this mess. Don't you think I wouldn't rather have him back—have them *both* back—have things like they were before, like they were meant to be—than any of this?' She made a sweeping gesture with one arm, encompassing the room, but its intensity implied the whole property. 'Don't you think I might wish he'd sold the hotel years ago, even to your family, if it would have given him a few extra years of peace? I wasn't here for him. I never even got to say goodbye...' She rubbed a hand across her face.

Matheo's voice was low when he spoke again. 'You went to say goodbye to your parents this afternoon. You could hate your father for leaving you with all this. But you don't.'

'No. And I can never make up for not being here. I can never make it better.'

'Do you want to talk about it?'

Talking about emotions was not something Matheo did. Not ever, if he could help it. But something about the way her eyes gleamed and the resolute way she straightened her shoulders made him say it. The little flame, which he now acknowledged was sympathy, flickered in his gut. He let it burn.

Cassandra stared at her fingers, knotted around

the mug. 'I always thought there'd be time. I knew my father was depressed. He'd been on medication for years, but I thought he was healthy enough. I imagined that one day I'd be able to have a proper conversation with him again. After my mother died, he changed overnight. He became obsessive about keeping everything exactly as it had always been, as if she might come back and expect to find it just as she'd left it.' She glanced up at him and half smiled. 'When you and your father turned up, the only time he'd spoken to me in weeks was to yell at me.'

'*Why?* What had you done?'

'I'd put on one of Mum's cardigans. I wasn't cold. I was just desperate to find a connection to her, to feel her presence, somehow. He told me never to touch anything of hers again. And I didn't, until after he died.'

'That's—extreme behaviour. You didn't deserve that.'

She shrugged. 'Maybe not. But it was his way of coping and I had to respect that. I had to force myself to go away to college, but I knew the staff would continue to run the hotel and look after him. They did, but there was nobody to authorise repairs or introduce new ideas. Things began to crumble. It's ironic that Nick and I were renovating boutique hotels successfully but were never allowed to touch this one.' She smiled. 'Don't you think?'

He nodded. 'Yes. But now?'

'It was only after he died that I discovered the true state of affairs. I took a year off from FuturePlan and came down here to try to put things right, although I've continued to go up to London when I can to keep up with what's happening. It was naïve, stupid, even. It was never going to work. FuturePlan is doing well—very well—but the cash flow doesn't allow us to put funds into this. I must sell it to pay off the debts.' She pulled up her knees and hugged them. 'It's a pity. We have such a great vision of how it should be.'

Matheo was way out of his comfort zone. He didn't want to hear any of this, but he'd encouraged her to talk and he now searched for a response. But before he could come up with one, she spoke again.

'So I've learned never to put things off. Never to think there'll always be another chance. There usually won't be.'

'Where were you? When he died, I mean,' Matheo asked on impulse. Her answer wouldn't matter to him, but he felt he had to say something and the dimness of the room made it easier to talk.

Cass swallowed hard.

'In India, on an ashram. I was on a buying trip for a project and I'd taken a few days' holiday at the end of it.'

Matheo nodded. 'So you feel guilty? If you

hadn't taken a holiday in India but come home to Cornwall instead…'

'Exactly. It probably wouldn't have made any difference. He would still have had the heart attack. But at least I would have been here.'

'What are you going to do now? Where are you going?' He put his empty mug on the floor and leaned back in the saggy chair.

'I need to get back to work. Nick has been incredibly generous giving me so much time, but there's a lot on. It's the end of an era for me but I know it's timely. In a way, the struggle over the past year has been good. It's been exhausting and dispiriting but it's allowed me to accept, gradually, that the hotel has to change. The debts, over which I've had nightmares for months, need to be addressed. It's time for me to move on and allow the Hideaway to move on, too. It can be reinvented for the future.'

'Do the debts include payments owing to the staff?'

He kept his eyes locked on her face. Its openness seemed to display her every emotion. He knew he was probing, just as he knew the staff were all paid up to date.

'The staff are all paid. I don't owe them anything.'

But his infallible business sense and intuition, which had helped propel him to where he was, suddenly shifted up a gear. He was sure that very close to the surface lay the solution to the imbalance in the figures he'd found.

The grip of her arms around her knees tightened and she stared at the floor, avoiding his eyes.

'I know,' he responded. He felt like a stalking predator, and he experienced a sudden distaste for the role. 'That's what I need to ask my accountant to explain. Every other part of the business is in debt up to the hilt, but you've continued to pay the staff, every month, on time.' He paused. 'Where has the money come from?'

Cassandra raised her head and returned his stare. 'I don't owe you any explanations.' Her whole body radiated defiance.

Not many people faced Matheo down when he was determined to get something they were unwilling to give but his lack of success with Cassandra was entirely his fault, he thought. Her mouth, with its full lower lip, was a major distraction and prevented him from focusing his full attention on what was important. He dragged his eyes away from her face and stood up.

She uncurled her legs and, in a fluid movement, rose from the sofa. Her baggy sweater did not disguise her slender build and he thought again about how her outward appearance of fragility masked an iron will and tough determination.

He took in the tremor of her bottom lip, slightly swollen from where she'd caught it in her teeth, and the tell-tale glitter of tears on her lids. She blinked them back and bit her lip again and a wary defiance replaced sadness in her eyes.

Nothing was going to make any of this okay and he hated the feeling that gave him.

She turned away from him, tucking her hands into her armpits. 'Please… I need to get some sleep.'

From the door Matheo glanced over his shoulder. Despite her attempt at bravado there was a vulnerability about her that tugged uncomfortably at an unfamiliar part of him.

And then he thought of something which might make things just a bit more okay.

'If you sell to me,' he said, 'I'll consider your proposal.'

Cassandra stared at the door as it clicked closed behind him. Had he really just said that? She shook her head, bewilderment whirling through her. She took two steps backwards and sat down, flinging herself against the back of the sofa and pressing her fingers to her cheeks.

Any hope of a good night's sleep had just been shattered. Did he expect her to feel happy, or grateful? Because she felt neither.

She pulled the tartan rug off the floor and wrapped it around her shoulders as cold began to seep through her, but it wasn't the sort of cold that a threadbare blanket could fix.

She felt trapped and threatened. If she accepted his offer, could she even trust him to stick to his word and consider the proposal she'd put to him, or would he walk away once he had possession of the Hideaway? Her stomach clenched at the thought. If he was anything like his father, his word would mean nothing. She'd trusted the last man who'd promised her something, before realising that when Jason said he loved her his love came with conditions; conditions she had been unable to fulfil.

Here was another man in a position of power, telling her she might be able to have something—something which was in his power to give or to withhold—if she did as he demanded. If she refused, she'd have to accept a lower offer, and probably be declared bankrupt. How would that affect her position at FuturePlan? And she'd relinquish all control over what would become of her loyal and beloved friends who made up the staff of the hotel.

But if she accepted? Would he follow through? And if he did, there was no guarantee that he'd sign FuturePlan to the project. He'd only said he'd *consider* it.

Panic bloomed in her chest, squeezing her ribs and making it hard to breathe. Her heart pumped uncomfortably fast. She'd promised herself—*vowed*—that never again would she allow anyone to dictate to her. She reminded herself that

Matheo could only have power over her if she allowed it. But she hadn't ever imagined what else might be at stake; the other lives which could be affected by a decision she would make.

She eased herself down onto the cushions, pulling the rug over herself, and stared at the ceiling. The sofa, which had always been comfortable before, now felt as if several bricks had been stuffed into it. In her head she heard Jason's voice, telling her she'd only ever amount to anything if she did as he said, behaved as he demanded.

Never again.

Matheo Chevalier wasn't Jason, but he was just as dangerous. He'd put her in an intolerable position. Her self-confidence, which she'd built with such care, now felt fragile and unstable. The idea of trusting him was terrifying. The thought of betraying her father's wishes was heartbreaking.

She had to talk to Nick.

CHAPTER FOUR

PEARLY GREY LIGHT was seeping across the sky when Cassandra finally dropped into a restless sleep, her exhausted brain churning on a useless treadmill of unanswered questions So when her phone alarm buzzed she struggled through layers of fatigue, her head aching and her eyes heavy. She pulled herself upright on the sofa. The clouds and rain had vanished, blown away by the gale, and the sea lay quiet beneath an opalescent sky, waiting for the touch of the sun to give it a rose-tinted colour wash.

Suddenly she needed to see the sun rise over the beach in the cove below the hotel, one last time. She stood, tugging at her crumpled clothes and raking her fingers through her hair. Then she twisted it up on top of her head and, searching her pockets, found a pencil to spear the untidy knot in place.

The door behind her opened and she swung round, all her senses on high alert, but it was not

Matheo Chevalier who stood there, fresh from haunting her dreams. It was Tess, looking wild-eyed and anxious.

'Cass! I went to your room but you weren't there, just the bucket on the bed and your suitcase on the floor. Are you okay?' She clapped a hand to her forehead. 'Sorry, stupid question. How could you be okay?'

Cassandra felt a rush of affection for her friend.

'No, you're right, I'm not okay, but I should be asking you that question, Tess. How are you?'

'Oh, Cass, I'll be fine. But you…'

'I'm going down to the beach.' She saw the look on Tess's face. 'But,' she added, 'I need to do this on my own.'

'Seriously, Cass, you look awful. When did you last actually *sleep*?'

'Thanks, Tess. You make me feel like a million dollars.' She smiled, her face feeling stiff and awkward. 'As for sleep, what's that?'

'Let me come with you to the beach, Cass. I won't talk, honest. I'll be really quiet. I just don't think you…'

Cassandra held up a hand.

'I appreciate your concern, Tess, but I want to do this by myself. And I'll be fine. You don't need to worry about finding my clothes in a neat pile at the high-water mark and a one-way set of footprints in the sand.'

'Are you sure, Cass? Please…'

'Quite sure, but thanks anyway. You're a brilliant friend. Now, I need to go, or the sun will rise without me there.'

The beach above the high-tide mark had dried after the rain, and a thin, crisp layer crusted its surface. Cass removed her boots, rolled up her jeans, then dug her toes into the cool sand. It tickled her feet and made her smile again. She spread her arms wide and turned in a circle, before heading down to where little ripples washed onto the shore, leaving a delicate tracery of foam behind them as they receded. The water was icy cold and she gasped as it swirled around her ankles. The air felt clean and rinsed after the rain and she took several deep breaths of it, wishing she could store it up for some time in the future when she knew she'd miss the taste and smell of the sea. She stooped to pick up a delicate shell, which gleamed with its own mother-of-pearl rainbow on the sand. When she straightened up, Matheo Chevalier was standing in front of her.

He was dressed for running, but bare-footed this time. Under his T-shirt his chest rose and fell in deep, even breaths, as if he'd finished his warm-up and was ready to tackle a marathon.

'You were right. About the weather, that is.' He glanced at the horizon, where the burnished rim of the sun had just begun to reveal itself. 'We're going to see the sun this morning, despite the rain last night.'

Cass's stomach tightened as his eyes locked onto hers. Her mouth dried. She tried to think of something to say but no words could get past her constricted throat. She wanted to drag her eyes away, but he kept her gaze in his steady stare, as if he held an invisible thread connecting them and was increasing its tension with every ticking second.

'Did you get any sleep in the end?' His words washed over her. She had to make a conscious effort to stop listening to the sound of his voice and concentrate on what he was saying.

'Not really,' she finally managed as her brain creaked into action. 'Your parting shot kept me awake.'

She was shocked by his sudden appearance. He must have been watching her, when she'd thought she was alone. A little lick of anger flared in her stomach. All she wanted was solitude, this one last time, on her beach. Only it might be his beach soon.

He nodded. 'I'm sorry about that. It was ill-timed, but I realised I might not see you again. Have you reached a decision?'

'No. I want to watch the sunrise.' She filled her lungs with the cold, crystal-clear air again. 'On my own.'

He inclined his dark head with the utmost gravity.

'Of course, Mademoiselle Greenwood. I apologise for intruding.'

He extended his right hand, and the thread tightened again, pulling her hand into his. His grip was cool and firm, hinting at a strength that filled her once more with that unnamed and uncomfortable longing. She felt the hard pad of his thumb move against the inside of her wrist, and her tummy hollowed. His free hand came up and rested on her shoulder, just where the curve of her neck began. She knew that beneath his thumb he could feel the hectic beat of the pulse at the base of her throat.

'I wish you *bon voyage*. I look forward to hearing your decision.'

As that thread tugged her closer to him, she could see the roughness of his unshaven chin, the cleft that was almost, but not quite, a dimple in his cheek. But mostly she could see the strong, straight line of his mouth. Her world had shrunk to this very small space and everything else receded into the irrelevant distance.

She thought he was going to kiss her and there didn't seem to be anything she could do to stop him. She didn't think she wanted to. Her blood thrummed in her ears as her lips parted in anticipation of the touch of his mouth. He smelled fresh and clean, and he exuded an energy that she desperately wanted to share. She wanted to press her face into his chest and just breathe his essence into her soul.

His lips, feather-light, brushed her cheek, and then he drew back. Her lids fluttered up and she saw he was frowning down at her, strong brows drawn together. A small sound escaped from her throat and a silver flame fleetingly lit his dark eyes.

She wanted to freeze the moment and stay in it for ever, so she wouldn't have to make impossible decisions. But she had to stop it. If even contemplating selling the Hideaway to him wasn't betrayal enough, wanting to kiss him would stamp a seal on her treachery that would stay with her for eternity.

But before she could push him away his hands closed around her upper arms. She felt dizzy and confused for a moment and then the world stopped spinning in crazy circles and snapped back into brutal focus.

What was she doing, standing ankle-deep in freezing water, wanting to kiss her worst enemy? She pulled away and stepped backwards, but he kept a light hold of her.

'I thought you were going.' The chill of the water had spread through her whole body.

'I will go just as soon as I'm sure you aren't going to fall over into the sea.'

'Why would I do that? I'm perfectly fine.' She shivered violently.

He lifted one shoulder, a wealth of expression in the spare movement, and then dropped his hands.

'You're sure you're all right?'

He moved away, out of the water, raking a hand through his hair. Then, nodding courteously, he turned and jogged off down the beach, picking up speed as he disappeared behind the rocks that curved around the side of the cove.

The smooth, controlled rhythm of his running was at shocking odds with Cassandra's jangling nerves. Her jaw began to ache with the effort of suppressing the bouts of shivering that kept attacking her. She would not, ever, acknowledge a need for Matheo Chevalier.

Her fingers strayed to her cheek, but she snatched her hand away and buried it in her pocket. Her limbs felt heavy, but she told herself it was the result of extreme tiredness. It was nothing to do with the adrenalin rush that had hijacked her mind and body and almost run away with them.

Had he been taunting her? Reinforcing his power over her, letting her know he'd soon have everything he wanted from her, if she needed the renovation project badly enough? She kicked uselessly at a little wave that washed around her feet and saw the pale shell she'd picked up earlier lying on the sand in the shallow water. It must have fallen from her fingers when she… Stopping her thoughts right there, she bent and retrieved it, turning it over in her fingers. Its perfect beauty soothed her a little and she tucked it into her pocket.

Let me remember the beauty, she thought, *not the pain and loss.*

She turned and walked out of the water, onto the sand, which now gleamed in the early morning sun. Shoulders hunched, she hurried to collect her boots, and then made for the rocky path that climbed up to the hotel lawns. The granite building loomed above her, dominating the landscape as it had done for centuries, the ancient slates of the roof shining like pewter.

Hoping to avoid seeing anyone, she hurried up the back stairs to her room to pack her few remaining things, forcing her mind into coping mode.

But later, when she'd said her tearful goodbyes, as the taxi pulled out onto the narrow lane, she was compelled to look back one last time. So in the future, if anyone asked her, she'd be able to say yes, she knew exactly how it felt when your heart broke in two.

Matheo jogged down the beach towards the rocks. He found his rhythm within a few strides and picked up speed. The rocks were his goal right now. Once past them he would try to clear his head, to think straight, when he knew she could no longer see him if she was watching. He needed to keep up his steady pace just in case she was. It seemed to take for ever, but eventually he knew he was hidden from her view. Even then, however, he didn't stop because if he did he'd turn and go back to her.

And then what? He slammed his mind shut. He didn't dare think about that.

His simple farewell kiss on her cheek had turned into something weightier, freighted with emotions he didn't want to explore.

Her scent, of rain and salt spray, lingered in his nostrils. And had that been a pencil skewered in her hair? A *pencil*? He'd been seconds from pulling it out, so that he could feel the mass of shiny dark waves, tumble through his fingers like liquid ebony.

Matheo ran to a stop, bent forward and braced his hands on his knees, breathing fast and sweating hard. He remembered the wild girl he'd encountered on this very beach fourteen years ago, and his heart twisted. She'd been sad and vulnerable, and his father had been determined to wrench her home from her; his father, who always got what he wanted, whatever it took, whatever damage he did. But, and Matheo experienced a bleak dart of satisfaction, his father would not get the Hideaway.

No, *he* would be the one to take Cassandra's home from her. It felt as if the dart had pierced his heart and the satisfaction withered and died. He'd tear what she loved best from her, just as his father had tried to do. But then he'd never see her again and eventually these feelings of regret and sympathy would fizzle out. He would not allow them to weaken him, make him vulnerable.

He straightened, swearing under his breath, then he plunged into the sea, gasping as the icy cold water hit his overheated skin. He ploughed on, deeper, and then dived into a wave, surfacing beyond it and striking out through the surf, hammering home his determination with every powerful stroke.

CHAPTER FIVE

CASS STOOD WITH her back to the room, gazing at the view of the city spread out beneath her. Behind her, Nick, her business partner, shuffled papers on the table.

'So that's the story, Nick,' she said, after a pause. 'If I sell to Matheo Chevalier, I'll be betraying all my father's principles and wishes. But potentially I, or rather *we*...' she turned to face him '...will have a shot at getting the contract to renovate the Hideaway, and the staff might be given a chance to keep their jobs.'

'And if you don't?' Nick picked up a pencil and rolled it between the palms of his hands. Cass knew it was one of his stress-busting techniques. 'What then?'

'Then I accept a lower offer. I can still try to negotiate but the company behind that bid is not known for its flexible approach or its imagination.' Cass pressed her fingers into her temples. 'And I'll be left with unpaid debts.'

'Has Matheo Chevalier even made an offer?

Because until he does…' Nick placed the pencil on the table and spun it in an arc with the tip of a finger.

'It came in ten minutes ago. It's very generous and it would clear all the outstanding bills.' She bit her lip. 'My lawyer was at pains to point that out.'

'Cass, I don't share your personal history with either the hotel or the Chevaliers so I can try to give you a balanced opinion. And from where I'm standing there seems to be no contest. The only question I have is, can you trust him to follow through on his promise to consider your proposal?'

Cass sat down at the table and propped her chin in her hands. 'I wouldn't trust his father, but I… I think Matheo is different. The lawyers have already emailed me a draft contract. It includes his undertaking to consider my proposal.'

'You know,' Nick said, carefully, 'that the project you were working on before your father died was completed last week?'

Cass nodded. 'I'm sorry I had to pull out of it. Really bad timing, but I'd been off the project for a year anyway, so…'

'You were responsible for the interior design, Cass. It all went ahead just as you planned it, and it's stunning. It's getting five-star reviews and it's been nominated for two awards. None of that would have happened without your input. It's a great shame you weren't able to see it through to completion.'

'Thanks, Nick. You're very generous, but what's that got to do with the predicament I find myself in today?'

'Looking at the situation objectively, it just might help you to make a decision. We're riding a wave of success at the moment. Other projects are progressing, but winning a contract from Matheo Chevalier would ensure our current high profile is maintained. He'd be the most important client we've ever handled. It wouldn't be a big contract for him, but if he likes what we do there'd be more work from him in the future. He's building a formidable chain of hotels.'

He crossed the room to stand next to Cass's chair. She folded her arms and stared out of the window. She felt as if every fibre in her body was stretched to breaking point, and even though Nick was obviously doing his best to appear relaxed, she could feel the tension radiating off him.

'Also,' he continued, 'renovating the Hideaway is what you and I have talked about doing ever since we started the company, isn't it? The way things are, this is the only chance you're going to get to do it, if we land the contract.'

Cass nodded. 'I know. It's just that this way I feel as if I'm being forced into it. You know how I am about coercion.' She smiled. 'Legacy of Jason, but I don't need to tell you that.'

'This is not coercion, Cass. Not by me, and not by Matheo Chevalier. It makes sound business sense to accept an offer that will clear your debts and potentially give you the two things you hope for from the sale. I can try to understand how incredibly difficult it must feel for you, given the history between your families, but I don't think your father would have wanted to see you bankrupted for the sake of an argument that goes back generations and for which there is never going to be a satisfactory outcome.'

Nick left her side and walked around the table to the window. Tense muscles stretched across his back.

'What you're saying,' she said quietly, 'is that it's a no-brainer. I should accept the offer.'

He didn't speak for a full minute, and then he shrugged. 'Yes,' he said. 'That is what I'm saying.'

Cass dropped her head into her hands and inhaled a deep breath. 'Thank you, Nick. I know you're right. I just needed to talk it through with someone, to get it all straight in my head.'

Cass walked towards the lift, fixing her gaze straight ahead, and when the doors swished apart she was relieved to find it empty. Her first goal was to get out into the anonymous London streets and find a lethally strong cup of coffee. Her second was to avoid talking to anyone else on the way.

With Nick's moral support she'd accepted Matheo Chevalier's offer for the Hideaway and now she was struggling to feel anything at all. She'd imagined this moment many times over the past few weeks, when she knew selling was inevitable, and she'd wondered how she'd feel. Devastated? Crushed? *Unburdened?* She felt none of those.

There was an emptiness inside her where anxiety and stress had lodged for so long, and she supposed it would eventually shrink to nothing or fill with something else. Would she eventually feel guilt for betraying her family or simply relief that her nightmare of a year had ended?

As the lift dropped towards the ground floor she grimaced at her image in its mirrored walls. All colour had leached from her face. The eyes that stared back at her were dark and troubled. But she squared her shoulders and issued a quiet challenge to her reflection. She may have once been fragile, but she reminded herself she'd had to learn to be tough to get to where she was now.

She'd taken the rest of the day off, to organise her flat and her wardrobe. Both had suffered from her long absences in Cornwall and were in urgent need of refreshing. Then tomorrow she'd be back at her desk, putting together FuturePlan's bid for the renovation of the Hideaway.

She would put out of her mind the way Matheo had made her feel when he'd kissed her goodbye in the sea. It had been nothing more than a simple farewell kiss, and anything more she'd read into their encounter had been the result of her stress, anxiety and lack of sleep.

She and Nick would gather a team which would throw everything at their bid. She owed it to the staff and to her parents to make a success of it. She may have lost the hotel to their worst enemy but, if Matheo would allow it, she could give it back some sparkle and shine to take it on the next stage of its journey.

Matheo Chevalier slowed his pace as he neared the end of the beach. *His* beach. On *his* island. It was a still spring morning with a freshness to the breeze that would take any heat out of the day later. Ripples of water caressed the pristine sand and further out the Mediterranean reflected the blue of the sky. Even the few wisps of white cloud were echoed by the froth of foam, dancing on the surface of the sea.

He gazed out at the perfection of the view but didn't see it. His thoughts had kept him awake for a large part of the night and he was frustrated and annoyed by that. On St Celeste he usually slept undisturbed, the quiet he found on the island providing him with the peace he craved. He knew it was said that he was becoming a recluse, but he didn't care. This was where he wanted to be, preferably alone, except for his loyal staff.

He'd grappled with the problem for hours, but as he waded into the sea to cool off after his run he decided what to do. As soon as he'd finished his swim he'd go to his office and send the email that would sort things out.

Since Wednesday last week, when he'd left Cornwall and flown in his private jet from Bristol to Nice, via a one-night stopover in London, his inbox had been cluttered with news and messages about the new hotel in the Western Isles of Scotland, called the Sandpiper. He'd heard of it over the past couple of years but never paid much attention. Now he wondered why.

It was stunning. He'd studied the pictures for hours, intrigued by the melding of ancient buildings and modern structures and the eclecticism of the interiors, where classic antique pieces of furniture sat beside new, modern designs, looking as if they were made to occupy the same space as each other. Natural light poured in through wide windows, but log fires warmed richly furnished nooks, where heavy curtains would keep the icy winter winds at bay. The attention to detail in the renovated building, the new extension and the layered interiors was astounding.

It had taken him no more than a few minutes to decide that this was how he wanted the Hideaway to be. He'd made up his mind and he was not known for changing it. He was anxious to get the project started.

Cassandra Greenwood had accepted his offer. He'd have been astonished if she'd refused it but he hadn't been sure of her. She was a businesswoman who could see the advantages in his bid, but at the same time the unresolved trauma of the loss of her parents and her home could have adversely affected her judgement. He admired her attachment to her roots and her reluctance to sever herself from them. He wished his feelings about his past were less conflicted. He seemed to have been trying to escape it for most of his life. But he was pleased Cassandra Greenwood had made the sensible decision.

Now he wondered if he'd been hasty in agreeing to consider her proposal if she sold to him. She'd probably have accepted his offer in the end, anyway. Her lawyer would have put her under pressure to do so, and Matheo could have saved himself a lot of trouble and several sleep-deprived nights.

Had he been right to allow his pity for Cassandra to affect the deal he'd done? Now that he'd bought the Hideaway, he should follow through with his promise. He'd had it written into the contract, but he could probably get out of it, if necessary. But it wouldn't be difficult to give the members of staff who wished it a chance to stay on. He could delegate that and need have no more to do with it.

The renovations were a different matter. He'd

decided he wanted the team who were responsible for the Sandpiper and he'd make sure he got it. He felt a rare frisson of excitement run through him at the thought of what they would be able to do with the Hideaway. But he'd promised he'd consider a proposal from Cassandra and… Nick? Was that her partner's name?

While coming to his conclusion he'd tried to be objective. He acknowledged the strange pull that seemed to draw him and Cassandra to each other but he rationalised it away. It was all down to their shared history; to the way they'd connected fourteen years ago, when he'd provided the listening ear she so desperately needed, having lost her mother to cancer and her father to all-consuming grief. The attraction she held for him must go back to that. It couldn't be anything else.

On his one-night stop-over in London, he'd driven up to the North London cemetery where he knew his mother was buried and searched for her grave. It had obviously lain untended since the day she'd been buried. He'd scratched the moss from the headstone with a fingernail and pulled up some of the brambles encroaching on it. Later, back in the suite he kept at Claridge's, he'd gone online to find a gardening contractor and engaged them to care for the site and make sure there were fresh flowers placed on it every week. Then he'd considered repeating the exercise, this time in Cornwall, for the graves of Cassandra's parents. But he decided against it. It would be high-handed and she wouldn't like that.

He walked out of the sea and back along the beach, enjoying the feel of the sun on his back, drying off the droplets of water, leaving behind a faint, sparkling trace of salt on his skin. He'd told Cassandra that if she sold to him he'd consider her proposal, and he intended to keep his side of the deal. He'd ask them to prepare a proposal and he'd arrange for them to travel to St Celeste to present it to him.

But he'd be completely honest and up-front about it. He'd tell them he'd already decided on another company.

Having made the decision, Matheo felt happier. He owned the Hideaway, at last, and he'd finish up with a spectacular boutique hotel in a matchless location. The deal had been a challenging one because he'd thought Cassandra might sell to someone else at any moment. But he'd kept his cool and eventually thrown her the bait he was sure she'd take. And she had.

What could possibly go wrong?

CHAPTER SIX

AFTER THE STABLE comfort of the big jet which had brought her to Nice in the South of France, the helicopter felt small and lightweight. Cass clutched the slim case containing her laptop to her chest and thought about the fact that she was about to meet Matheo Chevalier again. Would he be different on his own private turf? Less demanding? More…*forgiving*?

She wished, very much, that Nick had been able to accompany her. But he was tied up in pitching for another project and she was on her own.

It had only been a few days after the sale had gone through that Cass's lawyer had let her know that Matheo was honouring his side of the agreement and anticipating a pitch from FuturePlan. He'd given them an almost impossible deadline—he was obviously anxious to get the project underway.

At least the insane hours they'd had to work had taken Cass's mind off the sense of bereavement that had hit her two days after she'd accepted the offer. It was as if the loss of the hotel had been a catalyst for facing all the other losses she'd suffered. She'd pushed through the pain, working eighteen-hour days, refusing to dwell on the past. She thought their proposal was brilliant and she was prepared to push Matheo Chevalier to the brink to get him to accept it.

What she'd do if he turned it down she didn't know, because she hadn't allowed herself to think about that. Her vision for the refurbished Hideaway was so strong it filled her imagination to the exclusion of all else.

She felt tired, and anxious about what the next few hours would bring, but she was fired up with enough determination to get through almost anything.

The uniformed driver who'd met her would not have looked out of place on the bridge of a ship. He'd driven her a short distance across the airport to where a line of private jets and two helicopters were parked, and deposited her, with reserved deference, at the foot of a set of steps that led into one of them. The taciturn pilot had handed her a pair of ear defenders and they'd been airborne much too quickly. Now they were rapidly descending, even though all she could see in every direction was the deep blue of the sea. The craft dipped alarmingly as they changed direction and skimmed just above the glittering water. There was a flash of white sand, followed by dusty green vegetation, and then she could see a landing pad rushing up to meet them. The skids touched down with a gentle bump and the rap of the rotor blades slowed to a lazy slap and then stopped altogether.

Cassandra exhaled. The door opened to a waft of warm air, faintly scented with lavender, and she was invited to step out.

An electric buggy waited at the foot of the steps, her carry-on bag already on board. The driver greeted her with a half-salute. The vehicle buzzed along a winding path, bordered with lavender bushes, and stopped at a small timber bridge. The structure beyond it was so well designed and situated it was almost invisible in the surrounding trees.

'Your suite, *mademoiselle*. We hope it is to your satisfaction.'

Cass nodded. 'Thank you.' The sapphire sky and the twenty-four-carat sunlight were a dazzling combination. A light breeze fanned her damp skin, taking the edge off the midday warmth. The murmur of the sea was a soothing background to the tumble of crystal-clear water flowing over pebbles in the stream beneath the bridge in front of her. London felt a million miles away. Cornwall might as well have been on another planet.

Cass followed the driver as he wheeled her luggage across the bridge. He shouldered open the timber door and ushered her inside. He lifted her bag onto a wooden rack and made a sweeping gesture. '*Bienvenue à* l'Isle de St Celeste, *mademoiselle*. I trust you will find all your needs met. You will be collected in an hour.' He backed out, pulling the door closed behind him.

As Cass's eyes adjusted to the dim interior, she made out the marble gleam of a bathroom, cleverly designed with glass walls facing an internal courtyard where delicate ferns grew. At first glance she thought the living space had no walls, but then she saw they consisted almost entirely of bifold glass doors, which stood open. The space led onto a timbered deck where two sun loungers stood in the shade of the overhanging trees. A wide bed, swathed in misty netting, dominated the room and a cream linen sofa and a pale wooden desk completed the furnishings.

Wooden steps led from the deck onto bright sand, which sloped away to meet the aquamarine of the sea. Millions of diamonds appeared to dance and sparkle on the surface of the water.

Cassandra wanted to sprint across the beach into the sea and push the thoughts of her impending meeting with Matheo Chevalier to the back of her mind. She longed to feel the soft silk of the water caressing her skin and soothing her overactive mind. But there was no time for relaxing. He'd emailed a tightly timed schedule and their first discussion would be in under an hour. What a pity this piece of paradise would not be hers to enjoy for little longer than one night.

She contented herself with slipping out of her shoes and stepping down the steps to bury her feet in the warm sand, wriggling her toes and feeling the arches of her feet tickle. Then she turned her back on the seductive beach and retreated indoors to change. The persona she intended to present to Matheo Chevalier was very different from the one he'd seen in Cornwall.

The double doors to the conference room were closed but the member of staff who had escorted Cass through the remarkable building pulled one open. She had wanted to stop every few steps to appreciate some other new element of the design of it. Now she hesitated on the threshold, her courage suddenly faltering. A clutch of panic sent her heartbeat into overdrive and brought a sweat to her palms, causing the strap of her laptop bag to slide through her fingers.

The two-week deadline they'd been given for this pitch meant she'd used the long hours of work to bury the realisation that she'd been forced to sell her heritage to the highest bidder. She'd found it almost impossible to acknowledge the identity of that bidder, even to herself. Her ancestors, all of whom had vowed never to let the Chevaliers get their hands on the Hideaway, would not have believed what she'd done, whatever her reasons.

Now she was about to see Matheo Chevalier again, face to face, for the first time since she'd accepted his offer. He'd known she'd had no option. She'd been backed into a corner with no way out apart from doing as he demanded, and she'd sworn no man would ever dominate her like that again.

Would he gloat? Rub in the fact that she'd been the one to lose the fight that had endured for generations?

He could try, but if she was about to see him again he was about to meet her true self for the very first time. Those few days at the Hideaway had come at the end of a long year of physical and mental stress. She'd been crushed by the realisation she'd have to sell and then by the arrival of Matheo Chevalier, with his money, power and position of unassailable strength. She reminded herself that he could only humiliate her if she allowed him to. She had a successful business and a great future. And perhaps her pitch this afternoon would allow her to leave her mark on the Hideaway, even if it was no longer her home.

She straightened her spine, lifted her chin, and, taking a firm grip on her laptop bag, stepped into a lofty room filled with light.

A polished wooden conference table, contoured to suit the curved glass walls of the space, occupied the middle of the room. Sleek wooden chairs, upholstered in cream leather, were arranged around it. A screen dominated one wall, and views of the sea, through floor-to-ceiling glass, another. A huge seascape hung on the wall opposite the windows, reflecting, rather than competing with, the Mediterranean, which filled the view.

It was one of the few spaces she'd ever entered that took her breath away.

She looked around, trying to take in the details without looking awestruck. The combination of perfect, low-key fittings, superb craftsmanship and sheer quality of furnishings added up to an atmosphere of absolute but understated luxury. She knew how difficult it was to achievc that look. And what it cost.

Her attention was drawn to the far end of the room as another pair of double doors swung open. Cass watched Matheo Chevalier walk through them.

He was dressed in light-coloured chinos and a pale blue linen shirt, the rolled-up sleeves exposing his strong, bronzed forearms. He looked more relaxed, more accessible, than he had in the dark suit and tie in Cornwall. Even so, she instantly remembered how his presence dominated a room; how he *possessed* the space around him; even a space like this. His thick, dark hair looked damp, as if he'd just stepped out of a shower. Easy confidence radiated from every toned muscle of his body. She'd seen him own his own power and relish using it and she thought she was about to see it again.

In spite of the talking-to she'd given herself, the breath left Cass's lungs and refused to come back. Her tongue stuck to the dry roof of her mouth and her heart, brought under control a minute ago, began to hammer again. Surely everyone else in the room could hear it. Matheo Chevalier had been followed in by two other members of his staff, and one of them was busy repositioning a chair at the head of the table.

She dragged her eyes upwards from where they were fixed on Matheo's long-fingered hands, but her stubborn mind instantly returned to the memory of how they had circled her upper arms, steadying her so that she wouldn't overbalance into the sea.

His intense grey eyes did a quick sweep of the room as he walked towards her. She managed to suck a gulp of air into her screaming lungs and relax the vice-like grip she had on her bag. For a split second her brain said she was going to be okay.

Then his eyes landed on her.

She wanted to see the moment when he registered the difference between the Cassandra who stood before him today and the one with whom he'd sparred in Cornwall.

He missed a beat, but only one.

Was it surprise that darkened his eyes to that

impenetrable slate? His gaze drilled into her and she struggled to hold her nerve. He stopped in front of her.

Close up, she could see he'd obliterated whatever emotion he'd experienced on recognising her and his eyes now held an expression of calm welcome. A muscle flicking in his jaw was the only indication that he might be processing anything else.

He may have been wrong-footed for a nanosecond, but he was evidently supremely practised at not showing his feelings. She extended her right hand towards him.

'Monsieur Chevalier. It's a pleasure to meet you again.'

He took her hand and kept his eyes riveted on hers. And then he spoke, his French accent more pronounced than she remembered.

'Mademoiselle Greenwood. Welcome to St Celeste.'

Matheo Chevalier stared at the woman in front of him. His brain, so analytical, so quick, was having trouble computing this. Was he hallucinating?

His world had rocked crazily on its axis in the split second it had taken for his eyes to see her and his brain to recognise her. Something had slammed into the rock-solid plane of his stomach with the force of a tank, threatening to knock the air from his lungs, and the impact, real or imagined, almost stopped him in his tracks. It was only his relentless practice of self-control, his rigid refusal to ever show his feelings, that prevented him from exclaiming in surprise. He breathed in through his nose, and out again, and kept on walking towards her.

Perhaps she'd disappear as he got nearer, like a mirage in a shimmering haze of heat. The memory of her that had played on the edges of his imagination since he'd dropped a light kiss on her cheek, standing ankle-deep in icy water, bore no resemblance to this.

He stopped close to her, but she remained as solid and real as anything else in the room. Only now everything had retreated to the blurred periphery of his vision and she was all that remained in sharp focus. He could smell her scent and he wondered how it could still take him back to a cold early morning on a Cornish beach. She was offering to shake his hand and he wanted to reach out to touch her to make sure she was real, but he hesitated. Holding on to his sanity seemed hard enough, without feeling her warm, satin skin under his fingers, or even the glossy beauty of her hair.

He hauled his eyes from her face and looked at that hair. It was swept up in a neat chignon, smooth and tamed, and held in place by a clasp decorated with a pale gold seashell.

What's happened to the pencil?

The question hammered uselessly in his brain.

His eyes flicked back to her face and he thought he glimpsed uncertainty there, as though she'd like to put some distance between them. Then his gaze swept on, taking in her cream linen jacket, sculpted to accentuate her slender waist, and the hint of ivory lace edging a camisole, just visible in the V between the lapels. The narrow skirt was short enough to make a man wonder how much further those legs went, and her feet, last seen in scruffy trainers, looked perfectly at home in a pair of nude killer heels. They revealed the pearly gleam of polish on her toenails.

He'd told himself her faded jeans and fisherman's sweater couldn't hide her slender figure. That was true, but what they'd hidden were her subtle curves.

He shook her hand and unclenched his jaw, noting that Cassandra Greenwood looked calm and self-possessed. Adrenalin pumped round his body. He hadn't felt this...*confused*...for a very long time. Not since his father... But this was no time to let that memory rise to the surface of his brain. He didn't dare allow it any oxygen. Now was not the time for the coruscating anger that always accompanied it.

He folded his arms across his chest and wrapped his hands around his biceps in case they shook. Then he rocked back on his heels. He allowed his gaze to travel from Cass's toes, up her legs, over her torso, to her face. She had caught her bottom lip, glistening with a hint of tinted gloss, in her teeth, the only sign that she wasn't completely relaxed. He frowned and released his hands enough to tap his fingers in a pent-up rhythm against the muscles of his upper arms. He rolled his shoulders.

'Shall we begin?'

The air of the room hummed with tension. Cass wondered if he welcomed everyone pitching for his business in this brusque manner or if he especially wanted to unsettle her. She swallowed, her brain racing to decide how to respond to him. She'd expected a warmer reception, perhaps a preliminary chat. But if this was how he wanted the meeting to be, she'd roll with it.

She slid her laptop from its case and opened it, finding a socket set into the light wooden floor to plug it in. They'd printed a glossy brochure filled with computer-generated images of how their vision of the Hideaway would look and she slid a copy across the table to Matheo. At last his eyes left her face to look at the pages as he flicked through them. Then he dropped the book onto the table and indicated the two men at his side.

'Tim and Ben, two of my assistants. They'll help you to set up.' He settled into the chair at the head of the table and rested his forearms on its polished surface, his hands loosely linked.

Within a few minutes her computer had been connected to the St Celeste wireless network and the FuturePlan logo flashed up on the screen, faint in the bright daylight. This, thought Cass, was hopeless. They wouldn't be able to see anything of her presentation. There were no blinds or curtains at the vast windows so there appeared to be no way of darkening the room. She opened her mouth to speak but Matheo held up a hand.

'Before you begin, I need to tell you that I have already identified the company I intend to use for the renovations of the Hideaway Hotel.'

Cass stared at him, shocked. Then suddenly she thought she understood what was going on.

'There is no point to my presentation, then. This trip, in fact the past two weeks, have all been a waste of time. All you're doing is paying lip service to the contract. Is that all you ever intended to do?'

If he was surprised at her directness, he gave no sign. She remembered telling Nick that she thought they could trust Matheo. She'd been wrong.

'The relevant word in the contract is "consider". I said I would *consider* your proposal.' His voice was even, steady. 'As you probably know, I've fulfilled my obligations to the members of staff at the Hideaway. I said I would also consider allowing you to be involved in the renovations. I do not break promises. But I think it is only fair, and honest, to tell you that I have decided on the company I plan to employ to do the work.'

The instructions FuturePlan had received had been precise. The presentation would take place on St Celeste at three o'clock in the afternoon and the company's representative would stay the night on the island and take the first flight from Nice back to London the following morning. Perhaps, thought Cass, since there'll be no need for any post-presentation discussion, I might even make the last flight out this evening.

But she refused to be rushed. She and the team in London had spent long days and nights putting this together. She'd rehearsed it endlessly, up until the flight had touched down in Nice, going over answers to possible questions, making sure she had all the facts and figures in her head. She had no notes or prompts. She owed it to Nick and the rest of her colleagues at FuturePlan to give it her best shot. Even if Matheo Chevalier wasn't interested in their proposal, she was going to make sure he was impressed with their pitch, she thought, irritation at his high-handed manner shivering through her. She might never see him again after today, but she was determined he'd remember her.

In the years ahead, when FuturePlan was famous and their projects seen as some of the best, most sustainable and eco-friendly in the world, he'd wonder why he hadn't signed them.

She was about to switch her attention to Ben or Tim, to ask if there was any way they could darken the room, when Matheo inclined his head.

'The impact of your presentation, Mlle Greenwood, depends on you.'

'But if you've already made up your mind…'

'I have.' His eyes, flint-grey, held hers. 'So, change it.'

He nodded to Ben, who raised his hand to a panel of buttons set into the wall near the door. The window was transformed into darkened glass and the only remaining illumination in the room came from a few hidden low-energy lights at floor level.

Cassandra closed her eyes briefly, confident that any show of frustration or anxiety on her part would be hidden in the dark. She inhaled and exhaled deeply and quietly and pressed her hands together in her lap before moving her fingers to the touchpad of her laptop. She tried to relax her jaw and throat.

'Well, then,' she said, 'prepare to be amazed.'

CHAPTER SEVEN

AFTER THE FINAL image of the presentation had faded from the screen there was silence in the conference room. Cassandra let it grow. Then she clicked off her computer.

'Thank you,' she said into the quiet.

She heard Ben push his chair back and within seconds the darkness retreated from the windows and natural light poured in again. The sea glittered in the afternoon sun.

Ben placed a glass and a jug of water at her elbow. Ice clinked as she poured it and took several swallows. Her mouth and throat felt parched. She closed her computer and returned it to its case, before deliberately turning her head to look at Matheo.

He had relaxed back in his chair, his arms folded, and his narrowed gaze appeared to be trained on the horizon. If his expression hadn't been thoughtful, Cassandra would have decided he hadn't taken any notice of her presentation. Then, as if he felt her eyes on him, he turned.

'Even if I haven't changed your mind,' she said, 'I hope I've at least made an impression.'

The straight line of his mouth lifted on one side; the side where the almost-dimple indented his cheek. He nodded, leaning forward.

'Yes, you have.'

Cassandra felt her cheeks grow a little warm under his scrutiny. She gripped her hands together and dipped her head.

'Good. I'm glad. At least I'll be able to return to London and report that you "considered" our ideas.' She lifted the glass at her elbow and sipped at the water again, then glanced at her watch. 'And I think if I hurry, and your helicopter is available, I might be able to catch an evening flight home. There is little point in staying if we have nothing further to discuss.' She pulled the laptop bag off the table and slipped the strap over her shoulder, not wanting to look hurried, but desperate to leave.

'The arrangement was that you would stay the night on St Celeste.'

'Yes, I know, but under the circumstances...'

'Under the circumstances, there are questions I'd like to ask you. I found several points in your presentation intriguing. Obviously, you know the Hideaway better than anyone and you've put that knowledge to impressive use in this scheme.' He turned to study the view again. 'With a few alterations to the old building you imply you could bring in much more natural light, but not compromise the timeless quality of the interiors. Here, the light is an integral part of the building. It's an element in its own right. You can't deny its importance.'

'It's the quality of the light that's different. In Cornwall, it's clear but never harsh. That's why schools of painting were established at Newlyn and St Ives, and the work of artists who lived there is unmistakeable for the expression of natural light on their canvasses. The same is true of the Mediterranean, but it's a...*different*...light.' She took a breath. 'You can let Cornish light into ancient interiors and it will enhance them. Mediterranean light sits better with big, modern spaces, like this conference room.'

He nodded. 'Yes. None of the images appear over-lit or harsh.' His gaze, when he returned it to her, was thoughtful, softer. 'But neither does this room. I'd be interested to know more about how you develop your ideas.'

Cassandra's teeth fastened on her bottom lip as she considered his words. Was there a possibility she might have swayed him in their favour? She needed to pursue this line of discussion now, while the images and her descriptions were fresh in his memory and the impression she'd made still endured.

'I'm happy to answer any questions you may have. Now would be a good time as I could return to any sections of the presentation you'd like to see again.' She slipped the strap of the laptop bag off her shoulder and began to unzip the case.

His smile, when he unleashed its full wattage, was devastating. It reached his eyes, making them crinkle slightly at the corners, and confirmed that the indentation in his cheek was a proper dimple.

'I admire your enthusiasm and determination. But I have a conference call in,' he glanced at his watch, 'twenty minutes, and I need to prepare for it.' He pushed back his chair and stood up. 'However, I'd be pleased if you'd join me for dinner at eight, on the terrace, when we can continue this discussion. I hope you won't turn me down a second time.'

Cassandra's heart sank a little. She felt she had the advantage of immediacy and that could well be lost over the next few hours, especially if his conference call was with the company he'd already chosen. However, she couldn't report back to Nick that Matheo Chevalier had wanted to discuss their proposal further, but she'd opted to return home instead. And over dinner she might be able to ask him which company he'd chosen for the project. It was always useful to know the competition.

She pinned on a smile and nodded.

'The last time you asked me to dinner was not a good day. I might enjoy it more this time. As long as there is not spotted dick on the menu.'

His lips twitched. 'I can guarantee it. I can also guarantee that you'll be blown away by the view.'

The last time he'd asked her to dinner it had felt like a command; one which she could not obey.

This time it felt like an invitation.

CHAPTER EIGHT

DISAPPOINTMENT, HOT AND BITTER, hit Cass as soon as she closed the door behind her. She'd insisted she could find her own way back, and she had, hurrying along the gravel paths as quickly as her heels would let her, her bag banging at her hip. As long as she kept going she could hold her emotions in check, but in the dim privacy of her suite she let them engulf her.

When had Matheo decided which company to hire? Had he known all along? He said he did not break promises, that he needed to be honest with her. But if he'd let FuturePlan do all that work, if he'd been playing her like a fish on a line for his own entertainment, that was dishonest in its own way.

She dumped her bag on the floor and flung herself onto the bed, staring at the pale wooden ceiling, each joint perfectly dovetailed, each plank honed to a butter-smooth shine. Just another man, she thought. Just another man who couldn't be trusted.

Her phone buzzed with a message from Nick, consisting of a single question mark. She wanted to keep the disappointment to herself, not to spread it through the office in London, but she knew Nick and the rest of the team would be waiting, anxiously, for news. She sent him a brief reply, saying she'd see him tomorrow, with a more detailed explanation. She imagined their despondency; how the optimism that had kept them going would drain away and exhaustion would take over. She hoped they'd believe she'd done her best in a no-win situation.

Since she'd slipped down that ladder into Matheo Chevalier's arms she'd felt like a puppet with him tugging her strings. Now she felt as if the strings had been cut, along with any possible further link to her beloved Hideaway. All that lay ahead was a return to work. It was work that she loved, and she knew she'd quickly become absorbed by new projects, but she'd been so full of hope, for so many reasons, for this one.

Things that seemed too good to be true usually were, she thought, and she should have known that. Perhaps someone without her connection to the Hideaway would have seen at once that Matheo Chevalier had never intended to let FuturePlan anywhere near the project. Having made the leap and sold to him, she'd been blinded by the possibility.

She thought about the evening ahead—making conversation, answering his questions, doing her best to sway his thinking while knowing it was a hopeless task—and she wished she was on her way home.

She rolled over onto her tummy and propped her chin in her hands, looking out at the white sandy beach and the ripples washing ashore from the blue, blue sea, and suddenly she knew the one thing that would make her feel better was the beach. All of her life it had been her playground, the place where she relaxed or where she went for solitude or solace.

She slid off the bed, kicked off her sandals and rummaged through her bag to find the bikini she'd stuffed in as an afterthought. She hadn't anticipated having time for a swim, but now it seemed like a necessity. It would lift her spirits.

She yanked the clip from her hair and peeled off the linen jacket and skirt.

Minutes later, she was running over the warm sand to dive into the crystalline water.

It was cold and she gasped when she surfaced, then she rolled onto her back and floated, arms and legs spread, like a starfish. She closed her eyes and relished the sensation of the warm sun on her face and the water rocking her tired body. When she finally emerged, she sat on the sand for a few minutes to dry off, and then made her way back to the wooden steps to her terrace.

The powerful shower sent a cascade of hot

water pouring over her head and body, leaving her skin tingling. She wrapped herself in one of the soft bathrobes that hung behind the door and wondered what to do next. There were still three hours to wait before she'd have dinner with Matheo.

The lack of activity on her phone spoke silently of the massive disappointment she knew Nick must be experiencing. She was trapped in a frustrating web of luxury from which she longed to escape.

It was warm in the quiet dimness, and the hours of travel and accumulated short nights were taking their toll. The vast bed beckoned to her emotionally drained and physically exhausted body.

It was as comfortable as it looked. White linen sheets slid smoothly over her skin as she shed the bathrobe and slipped between them, surrendering to their soft caress. She might never again have the chance to be lulled to sleep by the sound of the Mediterranean Sea washing onto the sand, or the breeze whispering in the Stone pines.

Matheo finished his unsatisfactory conference call and switched off his computer. Perhaps he was tired. Perhaps he just wasn't interested enough in what the other guy had to say. Whatever it was, he'd found it difficult to concentrate and had had to ask him to repeat himself several times. Tim had sent at least one concerned glance in his direction, and after that had listened carefully, ready to prompt him when necessary. Now he was pretending to busy himself on his own laptop, as if he was reluctant to leave him, Matheo, on his own.

That irritated him further. He needed time and space to himself to try to resolve what was bothering him. But first he needed to work out exactly what that was.

Cassandra's presentation had been flawless. There seemed to be nothing it hadn't addressed, in as much detail as was necessary. She herself had been fluent, with strings of facts and figures at her fingertips. That she'd used no props, apart from the images on the screen, had impressed him.

Something about it, though, was catching at the periphery of his brain, but it was something he was finding impossible to pull into focus.

He didn't think it was the startling discrepancy between the exhausted and stressed Cassandra Greenwood he'd met in Cornwall and the cool, elegant woman who had waited in his conference room, ready to astonish him.

She had astonished him, on every level.

He'd been dragged back to that early morning, the smell of rain, the tang of salt, and the feeling of that tug, pulling him towards her. The memory of it was what had taken him back to the Hideaway in the first place, when he could have conducted the deal from the safety and comfort of this very desk. He'd tried to deny it, pushing it to the back of his mind, but he couldn't forget how the fleeting whisper of her cheek beneath his lips had driven him to run himself to a standstill. Only when he'd swum too far out to sea and then had to use all of his mental and physical strength to get back to the shore had he been able to shift her from front and centre of his mind, and then his respite was brief.

He wanted to sit across the table from her and see if he could unravel whatever it was that bothered him. His pulse had quickened when she'd suggested she might leave, needing to find a reason to persuade her to stay.

He told Tim he was going to the gym, but he found no relief from his thoughts on the treadmill or lifting weights. He showered and changed, then retrieved the FuturePlan brochure from the conference room and took it out onto his private terrace, but he couldn't figure out why he found the designs and ideas so beguiling. Irritation made him feel unsettled. He wasn't familiar with the feeling of being unable to solve a problem. There was still an hour to go before dinner. As his impatience grew, he flipped to the front of the brochure and began paging through it again.

Cass struggled up through layers of sleep and forced her eyes open. She lay still for a moment, her limbs heavy with lethargy, then she reached out for the light switch. It wasn't where it should have been. Instead, her hand encountered something soft and gauzy, which seemed to go on and on, in every direction. She shot bolt upright, panic clawing at her, and saw that, outside, dusk was rapidly dissolving into dark. Her brain creaked into action and the memories of the past few hours began to shuffle themselves into some sort of order. The soft murmuring of waves on the sand was not the Atlantic Ocean in unusually subdued mood. It was the warm Mediterranean. And that noise was not George hammering slates onto the roof that had blown off in a storm, it was someone knocking on her door.

She pushed her way through the mosquito netting and fumbled for the bathrobe she knew she'd discarded somewhere amongst the bedclothes.

'Just a minute,' she called, pulling it around her and trying to tie the belt.

The fog of sleep clouded her head. She couldn't think straight. She found a light switch and flicked it on in time to see the door handle turn and to remember that she hadn't locked it.

Matheo's deep, measured voice snapped her into full, wary awareness. Instinctively, she pulled the robe more tightly around her naked body.

'Mademoiselle Greenwood, were you asleep?'

Grave and seductive, his tone lent an intimacy to the words that caused her stomach to clench.

She tried to breathe, to banish any trace of anxiety or panic from her voice.

'Yes.' Was that the best she could do? Her voice was faint and breathy in her own ears, betraying the confusion and vulnerability she was trying to hide.

'It's past siesta time.'

'What time is it?'

'It's eight o'clock. In the evening.'

'*Eight?* I've been asleep for *hours*. I could've been almost home by now.'

He laughed.

'You could have. But you're having dinner with me, remember?'

'I was exhausted. I'd been travelling…' She stopped, remembering that she didn't need to justify herself to him.

'Forgive me for disturbing you, but you must be hungry.'

'I'm…sorry. I only planned a quick nap. If you'd rather cancel, that's fine…'

'Not at all. May I come in?' Without waiting for an answer, he stepped inside and closed the door behind him. 'The kitchen staff are waiting to serve dinner.'

Cassandra backed away, clutching at the neck of her bathrobe. 'I'm sorry,' she repeated, completely thrown off balance by his presence and her state of undress.

He strolled through the room, towards the terrace. 'I'll wait while you dress.' He nodded towards the bathroom.

She stood irresolute, not moving. 'I'm not sure…'

He glanced at his watch. 'Five minutes?'

He turned his back and stood staring out into the dark. Beyond him Cass could make out the pale glimmer of the sand and the shining black sheet that was the sea. In spite of his relaxed manner there was rigid tension across his wide shoulders. She wondered why.

She looked at the clothes in her cabin bag. When she'd packed, dinner *a deux* with Matheo Chevalier had not been on her agenda. She pulled out a rolled-up silk kaftan and a pair of loose linen cropped trousers and retreated to the bathroom.

Minutes later she surveyed herself in the mirrored wall. The lilac silk accentuated her eyes. She hoped it drew attention away from the dark circles under them. The dab of concealer that she'd applied had not done the job. She seemed to have lost her lipstick but found some gloss, which would have to do. Her hair was damp, but she twisted it up into a knot and fixed it with the shell clip she'd used earlier.

She closed her eyes and took a deep breath, exhaling slowly and mindfully, as a knock sounded on the bathroom door.

'Five minutes. Time's up.'

* * *

She'd probably keep him waiting another ten minutes. Matheo had folded his arms and leaned against the doorframe, so his guard was down when the bathroom door opened and Cass stepped out into the soft light of the hallway. The air left his lungs, and he struggled against an unfamiliar constriction in his chest when he tried to fill them again. He straightened, although he thought he might need the support of the door behind him if the effects of this adrenalin rush didn't ebb soon.

The diaphanous silk top she wore shimmered as she moved towards him, and the way it clung confirmed the memories he had of her body beneath it. Her direct gaze and fiercely determined air didn't quite mask the wariness shadowing her huge eyes. Her hair, which had been so tamed and smoothed earlier, had returned to its wilder state. A few tendrils had escaped from the knot held by the shell clip, and they curled against the creamy skin at the vulnerable-looking nape of her neck.

He thrust a hand through his hair. 'Shall we go?'

He turned the door handle, and she stepped outside, brushing against him. At the hint of her touch the unfamiliar tightness in his body, in which every muscle and sinew seemed to be under stress, wound itself up a couple more notches. He told himself it was because he needed to solve the problem that had plagued him ever since her presentation earlier this afternoon.

The sweet perfume of lavender and rosemary scented the warm night air. Tiny hidden solar lights glowed along the route of the winding pathway, although the glitter from the millions of stars in the velvet sky would have provided light enough. Cass looked up and marvelled at the jewelled depths of black space above her, wishing she could forget the disappointment of the afternoon and simply enjoy the place. She followed Matheo as he led the way towards the soft glow that shone from the island's main house.

Steps led up to huge glass doors set in wooden frames, though once through them it was difficult to tell if she was inside at all. The marble floor gleamed in the light of hundreds of lamps hanging from the trees and shrubs that grew in the atrium, their tops disappearing into the gloom above. Cass stopped to look around her. The clever use of natural materials and the spare, uncluttered design lent the space an otherworldliness. She felt she should tiptoe in her sequinned pumps to avoid disturbing anything.

Matheo strode towards the upward curve of a glass staircase, which seemed to float in the soaring space above them, among the palm trees. He waited for her at the bottom, and then looked down at her footwear.

'Slight design fault. Glass steps can be a little slippery.'

'You could have the edges of the treads sand-blasted. It would provide grip and would hardly be noticeable, amongst all this...beauty.'

'Thank you. I'm glad you like it. And that's a good idea. I'll remember it.'

He placed his hand under her elbow and guided her up the stairs. As they reached the top she eased her arm free again, and then almost wished she hadn't as the impact of the location hit her.

'Oh...wow...'

The bifold doors on the landing stood open and a polished wooden floor spread out onto a terrace bounded by a glass balustrade. The uninterrupted, three-hundred-and-sixty-degree view was jaw-droppingly, breathtakingly incredible.

White sand glimmered in the starlight, lit by lights hidden in the shrubs and plants on the fringes of the beach below them. Ripples, glowing with phosphorescence, crumbled their foam onto the wet shore and then sucked back with a soft sigh. A balmy breeze hissed through the leaves of the pines and the marble-black sea shifted restlessly, the only break in the horizon a smudge of light beginning to spill over its lip as the moon inched its way into the spangled sky.

In the other direction, the lights of the coast blinked and shimmered in the distance.

Cass stood rooted to the spot, trying to absorb

the beauty and at the same time catalogue all the design features that gave the space such a feeling of wholeness and of fitting so exactly with the surroundings.

'Would *mademoiselle* care to be seated?'

A waiter hovered at her elbow. He led the way towards Matheo, who stood at a table near the edge of the terrace.

Candles in glass lanterns flickered all around them. She sank onto soft cushions, still gazing around wide-eyed in every direction, trying to commit the details of the scene to memory. She wanted to take photographs, but it was Matheo's private space and he was a very private man.

Matheo took his place opposite her, his appraising gaze fixed on her face.

'What do you think?'

'It's one of the most beautiful places I've ever seen.'

'And your professional opinion?'

She looked around, finding it difficult to be objective and analytical.

'It's exquisitely designed and decorated. It blends seamlessly with the surrounding landscape and there is not a single jarring note. The use of timber and glass is inspirational.' She lifted her shoulders. 'Why are you employing another company for the Hideaway? Just use whoever did this.'

'With such a location,' his outstretched arm

encompassed the bay below them, 'the brief was simple: the building must not argue with what's here already. As far as possible, it needs to disappear. Sites like this are rare. They merit special attention.'

He reached out and poured water into a tumbler in front of her, ice clinking against crystal.

'With a site like the Hideaway,' he continued, 'you could knock the building down and...'

'No, you couldn't.' She spoke too quickly, so stopped and took a sip of water. 'I mean because it's listed,' she finished.

His cheek creased as a corner of his straight mouth lifted and she felt a flush stain her cheeks.

'I'm aware of that. I was going to say you could knock it down and build something dramatic and modern, but it would argue with the landscape. The Hideaway has been there for hundreds of years, and it's evolved over time, just as the landscape has. Why try to make a bold new statement when the existing one speaks loudly enough for itself?'

Cassandra tried to absorb this. His words mirrored her opinion exactly but hearing them from him disconcerted her. Unexpectedly and against her will she felt the solid rock of her dislike of all he stood for shift.

'But all your hotels—all the dozens of them across the world—are in a similar mould.' She wrapped both her hands around her glass of water and met his gaze. 'I know from experience a certain type of customer values that. Some people don't like to be challenged by their surroundings. Familiarity gives them security. The Hideaway will be different.'

'That is true, but while my hotels might all be similar, each one is individually designed and styled to make the most of the site and to appeal to the projected guest profile. After all, why check into a hotel in Gstaad that feels the same as one in Singapore?'

The waiter appeared; white linen was swathed around a bottle beaded with condensation.

'White wine, *mademoiselle*?'

She nodded and watched the pale liquid splash into her glass and then into Matheo's.

He lifted one powerful shoulder. 'My global brand delivers the emotional security guests like, with touches of individuality. Wherever you are in the world, the standards are equally high. Guests can relax knowing their expectations will be met, but unique features will always reflect the surroundings, link them to the landscape.' He nodded his thanks to the waiter. 'However, the Hideaway is a new departure for me. Something more individual and…intimate.'

He raised his glass and tilted it towards her. 'Mademoiselle Greenwood.'

Cassandra sipped at the wine, eyes on his lean

fingers where they gripped the stem of his glass. She tried to focus on what he was saying.

'Your ideas for the Hideaway intrigue me. I've been pondering them for the past few hours.'

Cassandra took a deep breath, placing her wine glass carefully on the table.

'Are you saying I managed to change your mind?'

He shook his head, crumbling her hopes.

'No. I'm wondering where they originated. Have they evolved over time, through all the years you've lived there? Or have you studied other projects, other designers, and taken inspiration from them?'

Cassandra took time to think about her answer, wanting it to be as accurate and truthful as possible.

'They've mostly come,' she said slowly, 'from my own very personal experience of living there. But I wouldn't have had those ideas if I hadn't studied interior design and worked with architects on other projects. It's difficult to separate the two elements. It's just something that...happens. And when it feels right, it usually is.' She could see he was listening intently. 'Could I ask *you* a question?'

A bowl of chilled soup had appeared in front of her. She took a piece of bread from the basket on the table and began to pull it to bits.

He leaned forward, interest sparking in his

eyes. 'Of course. But that bread is meant to be eaten, Cassandra, not shredded.'

Listening to the slightly accented syllables of her name rolling off his tongue made her pause. The sound stirred a memory of running down a beach, his voice on the wind…

'Does our proposal resemble, at all, what you imagine the Hideaway could look like? And how similar is it to the one by the company you've chosen?'

He nodded. 'Yes, and no. Yes, I imagine the Hideaway being very like the proposal you presented. And no, because I don't yet have one from the company I…think… I've chosen.'

'Well, then, how do you know you'll like their work? Who are they?'

Matheo looked away, over her shoulder towards the sea. 'I've become aware of a new hotel, which has opened to great acclaim. The pictures on the internet are incredible. Somehow, they reflect exactly the vision I have for the Hideaway. I haven't read enough yet to discover who was behind the project—it's been a busy time—but it only took me a few moments to decide I want to hire them.'

'Were those few minutes quite recent? Or have you known all along you weren't going to hire FuturePlan? Were you simply fulfilling the terms of the contract?' She sipped at a spoonful of the iced gazpacho.

'While that is irrelevant, it was nevertheless a few days ago.'

'It is not irrelevant to us. Our team put huge amounts of time and energy into getting the bid ready in the tight timeframe you gave us.' Her voice dropped. 'And I made a decision to trust you.'

'It is irrelevant because whatever had happened, I would have considered your proposal. I had made you a promise and I never break promises. Not ever.'

'I'm not sure that makes me feel any better, but I appreciate your honesty.' Cassandra tipped her head back. 'But what if,' she continued, gazing at the millions of stars, 'what if they don't want the project? What then?'

He looked at her, his dark brows pulled together. 'They'll want the project. Everyone wants my business.'

It sounded arrogant but Cassandra knew he was right. His name, wealth and influence packed a huge punch. Everyone wanted a part of it. Of *him*. And she was no exception.

'Well, assuming you're right, what's drawn you to them?'

'An element of originality, based firmly in traditional principles. It's hard to define. The best I can do is to ask you to apply your ideas for the Hideaway to a different project and see what you'd come up with. It's…' He shook his head. 'It's difficult.'

With those words, something fell into place in Cassandra's brain. She almost heard the click. She swallowed the bread she'd been chewing and put down her spoon on her plate. Gripping her hands in her lap, she scrunched the linen napkin into a tight ball. Her pulse quickened, so much that she thought Matheo might see it jumping at the base of her throat. She tried to control her breathing as it threatened to become shallow and unsteady.

'What,' she asked quietly, holding his gaze, 'is this project called?'

'You might have heard of it,' he said. 'It's in the Western Isles of Scotland. It's called the Sandpiper.'

CHAPTER NINE

MATHEO WATCHED CASSANDRA'S eyes widen. He'd never worry about drowning in the sea again. Those eyes would do for him right here at the table. A faint flush spread across the skin of her cheeks and then the colour drained away, leaving her pale. Her lips parted and then her teeth nipped on the bottom, fuller one.

'Mr Chevalier… Matheo…'

'Is something wrong? Are you ill?'

She shook her head and reached for the tumbler of water. He noticed that her hand shook slightly. He tried to think what had upset her. She'd asked the name of the hotel in Scotland.

'No. I'm not ill, thank you. Just…surprised. You see, that hotel…the Sandpiper…is the most recent project FuturePlan has completed. Those designs were done by Nick. The interiors are mine.'

A combination of shock and astonishment hit him. His first reaction was to deny that she could be right, but he stamped on that at once. Cassandra wouldn't make up something like this. What would be the point? And she couldn't be wrong. Unless there was another hotel of the same name. It seemed highly unlikely.

He sat back, keeping his reaction under control, hidden, behind a frown.

'Are you sure you're not confusing it with another hotel? And if you've been at the Hideaway for a year, how could those designs be yours? You haven't been closely involved with the project, obviously.'

Her laugh sounded a little unsure, but her eyes now glowed with excitement.

'There is absolutely no doubt. The hotel opened last week. It's true I wasn't involved with it for the time I was in Cornwall, but the designs were all completed before I took time out at the Hideaway. They're mine. You would have seen echoes of them in the presentation this afternoon. It's my style you recognised.'

The puzzle that had been snagging at his brain all evening suddenly resolved itself. The colours, the ancient stonework buildings, the clever uses of timber and glass, while unique, bore a similarity of style, which he now saw clearly.

He felt confused. Where did he go from here? It was obvious that Cassandra and the team at FuturePlan, when they heard about this revelation, would expect the contract to be theirs. It was the only honest way to proceed. He examined his feelings and had to admit to himself that the reservation he felt stemmed from the idea of having to work with Cassandra.

She was no longer that damaged girl he'd met years ago, or the woman with fierce determination in her blue eyes who had fought to keep her home and then fought to have a say in its future. He'd come up with a fair way to ensure she sold to him and he'd fulfilled his side of the bargain.

The Cassandra who had turned up in his conference room this afternoon was a different person altogether. Professional, polished and supremely well-prepared to push him into a decision in her favour, she'd impressed him more than he'd ever expected possible. He'd thought before that she was the sort of person he liked to hire, and those thoughts were coming back to bite him now.

Because he wasn't at all sure he could work with her. Her presence unsettled him, testing all the self-protective barriers he'd put in place. Her eyes would find a weak spot, her laugh another. Before he knew it, he'd allow that thread to tug her closer, and then it would snap…

But he saw, very quickly, that there was no way out of this. No honest, honourable way.

St Celeste was where he felt protected, safe. He trusted his staff and nobody came to the island without his knowledge. If, he thought, his brain running ahead of itself, he asked that Cassandra stay here to work with him on the scheme, he'd feel happier about giving the contract to Future-

Plan. That way he could control their interaction and keep himself informed of what was happening. If he felt his defences wavering, he could send her back to London at a moment's notice on some pretext.

It would only be for a few days, while they established the basics of what he wanted. After that it could all be done remotely.

Cassandra was watching him, her eyes bright with excitement. This meant so much more to her than just another job. He'd be giving her the opportunity she'd craved. Perhaps winning the contract for FuturePlan would compensate, in a small way, for her loss of the Hideaway. He'd wanted to make it all feel better for her and now it looked as if he could.

'Obviously,' he said, eventually, 'this puts everything in a completely different light.' The waiter placed plates of perfectly braised chicken in front of them, with an accompanying bowl of bright steamed vegetables. 'If what you say is…accurate… I see no reason why the contract shouldn't go to FuturePlan. I'd need to see your presentation again, to clear up a few points…'

'That's no problem. Perhaps tomorrow morning, before I leave?'

Matheo decided to put off the issue of her leaving until he could discuss it with her and her partner at the same time. Now he raised his glass. 'To the future of the Hideaway, Cassandra.'

She tilted her glass towards him, giving him the full benefit of her smile. 'My father always said if your family got their hands on it, they'd obliterate the hotel and build some hideous modern construction in its place, so it's a relief to know our ideas for its future are similar.'

Matheo dipped his head, the hard planes of his face emphasised by the shadow that fell across them. His mouth compressed.

'Your father had a low opinion of my family. The feeling was mutual.'

'We both know that. Selling to you was one of the most difficult decisions I've ever had to make, despite the deal you offered.' She spooned vegetables onto her plate. 'But now I think it was the right one. I spent a year trying to save it, but I slowly came to accept that the only way to really salvage it was to sell it, hopefully to a sympathetic buyer. I never expected it to be a Chevalier.'

'But you know we've wanted it for decades.'

'Oh, I know you wanted it. I just didn't expect you to be sympathetic to my wishes for it. I thought you and your father would want to remove all trace of us.'

'My father possibly would.'

'Are you going to be able to persuade him?' A shadow clouded her eyes. 'I've just realised working with you will mean working with him. I don't know if I can do that.'

He saw the knuckles of her hands turn white with tension as she gripped her knife and fork.

'As I've said before, my father has nothing at all to do with my purchase of the Hideaway. Marine Developments is my own company. He has no part in it.'

'I chose not to believe you. You seemed to be so like your father, although when we first met you weren't. Not at all. What's happened?'

'Let's just say our methods made us incompatible business partners, which means you won't have to work with him. He'll be angry when he learns I've bought the Hideaway, but that's my problem, not yours.'

He sat back and took a mouthful of wine.

The risen moon now painted a silver path towards the shore, and Cassandra wondered what the little cove below the Hideaway looked like tonight. Was the moon visible or was it, as more often than not, obscured by clouds scudding across the deep Cornish sky?

'As the people who had the original disagreement have long-since died, I don't understand how you can find buying it satisfying, or why it should bother you father.'

'My father never gives up until he gets what he wants, so, yes, he will be angry. As for my motives, revenge, they say, is a dish best served cold.' He dropped his gaze, wrapping his fingers around his wine glass.

Cassandra felt a cold fist close around her heart. 'Are you saying this is revenge against your *father*? I thought...'

'It's a personal matter. I don't care to discuss it.' His tone was sharp.

Cassandra bit her lip. 'It's just...family is so important...it seems such a waste...'

'Every family is different. Mine is...dysfunctional. That seems like a good word to describe it.'

'Another thing that's said—' Cass dragged her eyes away from his fingers and fixed them on his face '—is that the best revenge is to live your best life. That's what I plan to do.'

Matheo raised an arm and gestured towards the sea, the island, the beach. 'Perhaps this is my best life?'

'It's hard to imagine a better one. But isn't it sometimes lonely amid all this...perfection?'

Matheo leaned back in his chair and folded his arms across his chest.

'Never. But since you're here, invading my privacy—' he smiled '—and FuturePlan is going to be working for me, there is something I'd like to ask you.'

'I think I've told you everything there is to know about the Hideaway.'

'Perhaps not quite everything. This afternoon I received the report I'd requested from my forensic accountant.' She was aware of how closely he was watching her. 'He's good—very good—at what he does. But he has been unable to solve the mystery of how the staff of the Hideaway were being paid. And I wonder if you would care to shed any light on it.'

Cass caught her bottom lip in her teeth and looked down at her hands. She wondered what he knew. Was he trying to trick her in some way, to see if she'd tell the truth? And what use could the information possibly be to him? He owned the Hideaway now, including any remaining debts, but there were no debts on the staff payroll.

'Why does it matter? It makes no difference now.'

'You're right. It doesn't. But I don't like mysteries and I'm curious to discover the answer, if you'll share it . You must know it.'

If she didn't tell him the truth now, he'd find out some other way. She sighed out a breath.

'It's nothing sinister. Like your relationship with your father it's a personal matter, which I've chosen never to discuss, but I don't see that it matters now.' She looked at the uneaten food on her plate and felt her appetite fade. Remembering how she'd struggled to keep everything afloat, to ultimately lose control of it, made her feel sad. Although the outcome was a good one for the hotel, the staff and even for herself, she suddenly felt tired. The rush of excitement associated with getting the contract had drained away. She longed to slip into that comfortable bed and give herself up to sleep, and the quickest way there was to tell Matheo what he wanted to know. 'A trust fund was set up for me by my grandfather. He was a mining magnate and I was his only grandchild. I gained access to it when I was twenty-five.' She tucked an escaped tendril of hair behind an ear. 'I invested some of it in the partnership with Nick when we started FuturePlan. I planned to sell my flat in Camden and buy a house with a garden. Luckily, I hadn't got round to doing that, as I've been able to use it to pay the staff wages for the past year. They were due paid holidays, too, and some hadn't always been paid in the past, so I made up the arrears. But it's almost all gone. So maybe you coming along when you did was my lucky break, after all.' She smiled. 'Did you ever dream that one day you'd be cast in the role of the good guy?'

She held Matheo's stare. Then he shook his head slightly and seemed to make up his mind.

'I consider that,' he said, 'to be an incredibly kind and generous thing to do, but also a perfect example of throwing good money after bad.'

'You're probably right, at least about the good money part. And considering the state of the finances I inherited with the Hideaway, I accept your point. But perhaps you've never needed a job, or been responsible for another soul, whether it is your elderly mother or your cat.'

She was right, of course. He had no idea at

all. No one else had ever relied on him and he'd never had to fight for anything. Except once, and he'd lost that battle in the most humiliating way. He dragged his mind back to the present and the calm resignation of her expression.

'All I was doing,' she went on, smoothing out the white linen napkin she'd scrunched up in her fists, 'was trying to ensure people kept their jobs for as long as possible. I tried to encourage them to look for other opportunities, but no one wanted to listen. They seemed to think if we all tried hard enough things would work out.'

'I spoke to some of the staff after you left. I was trying to get an idea of how they'd react to my plans if you accepted my offer.'

'Which you were confident I would.'

He nodded. 'Yes. Fairly confident. Anyway, they all hold you in extraordinarily high regard, you know. They're fiercely loyal to you.

That kind of loyalty and affection is rare. And enviable.'

Cassandra took a deep, deep breath.

'Thank you.'

Matheo rested his folded arms on the table. He leaned towards her.

'George was especially robust in his praise of you.'

'George? I thought he resented all the repairs I asked him to do, when he'd rather have been growing vegetables.'

'He told me you'd encouraged him to concentrate on growing crops for the kitchen, but he felt the demands of the old building were more important. Your leaky bedroom was of great concern to him.'

'He kept me going sometimes, when I was ready to give up.'

'As soon as you accepted my offer I had Pierre, the interim manager, sort out the staff issues. I can forward his report to you. But in the meantime, I can tell you that George will spend the time during the renovations establishing a vegetable and fruit garden that will hopefully provide for many of the hotel kitchen needs.'

'That's such good news. ' She smiled at him. 'I never thought I'd be grateful to you for anything you did at the Hideaway.'

Cass lifted her eyes from her plate of food to look at him. There was a silver gleam of triumph in his eyes and she knew she'd misjudged him. In fact, she'd misjudged him long before he'd set foot in the Hideaway. But history had dictated what he'd be like, and until now history had been deadly accurate.

She took another mouthful of wine and noticed that her glass had been filled again. Suddenly, she felt light-headed and dizzy, and put the glass down.

'Are you all right?'

She shook her head. 'I just haven't eaten properly today.'

He indicated her plate. 'Well, this is better than anything you'd have got in the economy cabin of the red-eye flight back to London you wanted to catch. I fly the chef from a Michelin-starred restaurant on the Riviera over, when necessary.'

'Of course you do.'

He laughed. 'Ask him, if you don't believe me. He loves to discuss his dishes with guests. And if your plate returns to the kitchen untouched, he'll be out here to discover why.'

Cass took a mouthful of food. The knot of anxiety which had been a permanent fixture in her tummy for weeks had loosened.

'This will make up for the apology for a snack I'll be served on the flight home tomorrow,' she said.

Matheo stood at the glass balustrade on the edge of the terrace. It had been past midnight by the time they'd finished their meal and Cassandra had declined coffee.

He'd watched anxiety fade from her features and a new strength and positivity flow into her as she'd realised the renovation contract would go to FuturePlan and absorbed his information about the staff of the Hideaway. It had given him inexplicable pleasure. He examined the feeling and savoured it. Was this how it felt to be responsible for someone's happiness and to be able to make things better?

They were two professionals with similar ideas about a project close to both their hearts, for different reasons. He was glad he'd bought the failing hotel, even if his motivation had been flawed.

He pushed himself upright and decided to draft an email to Nick and Cassandra, setting out his requirements for the next few days.

Sleep, always elusive for him, felt impossible tonight.

CHAPTER TEN

MATHEO LOOKED UP to see Cassandra striding across the terrace towards him. She wore a cream linen shift and chic sunglasses, and her leather satchel swung from one shoulder. He flipped his laptop closed and stood up.

The morning breeze had whipped up frothy white tops to the waves and it snapped at the edges of the broad umbrella which shaded the table. It briefly flattened her dress against her body, teasing a tendril from the glossy ebony braid of her hair.

'Good morning.' She dumped the bag next to a chair and sat down, pulling out her laptop. 'Why didn't you discuss it with me first?'

Matheo frowned and decided the flush on her cheeks and her sparkling eyes were not the result of sunshine and the sea breeze. She was angry.

'I sent the email to both of you.'

'Yes, but you sent it at some unearthly hour of the morning. Nick is an insanely early riser and the first thing I knew about it was my phone buzzing in my ear and Nick saying it was a good idea for me to stay on here for a few days, because it's what you want.' She stared at him, her eyes flashing. 'I didn't know what he was talking about. I felt like a total idiot.'

The loose lock of her hair brushed across her face and she swiped at it with a hand that trembled.

'I'm sorry. I didn't mean that to happen.' He sat down opposite her and removed his sunglasses, dropping them into the top pocket of his shirt. 'I often work late and I needed to get the points down in the email while they were fresh in my head. If anything, I thought you'd read it first.'

'You must have already had the idea when we were having dinner. You could have mentioned it then.'

He nodded. 'I did think of it last night, but you were tired and I thought you might not be in the frame of mind to consider my suggestion.'

'Mr Chevalier. Matheo.' She replaced her shades. 'If we are going to work together you will have to agree to treat me as an equal, to Nick and to yourself. Nick and I are partners. You are our client. Please don't make allowances for me that you would not make for anyone else.' It sounded as if she was forcing the tremor out of her voice by sheer willpower.

'I apologise.' Matheo picked up the cafetière of fresh coffee. 'I should have discussed it with you first, or at least waited until this morning to send the email. It was a misjudgement on my part. Coffee?'

Cassandra sighed out a breath and her tense shoulders dropped. She surveyed the table.

'Yes, please. Mmm… Almond croissants are my absolute favourite and the coffee smells amazing.'

Matheo pinched the bridge of his nose, not convinced that her anger had subsided. 'Did you sleep well?'

She nodded. 'Yes, until Nick phoned. And, thanks to that wake-up call, I've already done some work.'

'*Work?*'

She pushed her sunglasses onto the top of her head, opening the computer. 'Do you have a problem with that? I had some newideas about the Hideaway after our discussion last night, and I thought I'd get them down while they were fresh in my mind, just in case you'd like to use them.' She clicked a couple of keys. 'Do you want to have a look?'

'Yes, I'd like to see them. Very much.' He ran a hand over the back of his head. 'But first, what did you say to Nick?' He felt tension wind up in his body. Her answer would shape not only the next few days but also the way the rest of the project would progress. If they could build an understanding from the beginning, face to face, running it remotely from St Celeste would be that much easier.

Cassandra adjusted the angle of her screen.

'I said "no". I'm annoyed that you just assumed I'd do as you want. I've only just returned to work after a traumatic year, which didn't end well. As you know.' There was pain in the look she flashed at him. 'I've spent two weeks working against a frankly unfair deadline. I have a life, both at work and at home, to be getting back to.'

'It would only be for a few days, but obviously if that isn't possible I'll understand.' Disappointment crept over him. He realised he'd done exactly what she accused him of. He'd assumed she'd stay, because he wanted her to, and his mind had already leapt ahead to the idea of sharing a few days with her. Apart from discussing the project, he was beginning to enjoy her company. If he got to know her a bit better, away from the emotional landscape of the Hideaway, if he found what made her tick, the whole project would run more smoothly.

Across the table, some of the tension seemed to drain out of Cassandra.

'I said "no", but then we discussed it more sensibly, when I'd woken up properly and actually read your email, and we've agreed I should stay until Friday. That gives us four days, which should be enough to start with.' She turned her head and looked out at the sea, breathing in deeply. 'It's a wonderful place to work, obviously, but…'

'But what?' Anxiety tugged at him. Why wouldn't she be happy to stay? Was it that she couldn't bear to be near to him, with their history of antagonism? He'd be able to empathise with that. He'd won the battle over the Hideaway but perhaps she wasn't ready to concede the war.

The thought that she might never be ready caused uneasiness to twist in his gut.

'It's so exquisite. The surroundings could be seriously distracting.'

Matheo relaxed into his chair and smiled.

'Thank you,' he said, pouring coffee into her cup, 'for agreeing to stay. I must learn not to fire off emails at three o'clock in the morning. After breakfast I'd like to go over your presentation again. The room will be dark. No distractions.'

Hours later, Cassandra settled down to work at a table on the terrace of her suite, but she found her mind wandering from the plans for the Hideaway. The restless sea kept pulling her gaze away from the notes in front of her, reflecting her equally restless thoughts.

The time spent with Matheo had flown by.

When Nick's call had dragged her from sleep early this morning, she'd been confused and then furious. Now she smiled at how Nick had talked her down from her panicked response. He'd had practice at it, over the years, especially in the early days of their partnership, when her break-up with Jason, and the reasons for it, had been raw. He'd prompted her to seek help from a therapist and just knowing he understood enough to make the suggestion had helped.

He'd suggested she read Matheo's email and reminded her that he was reclusive and perhaps not comfortable with unfamiliar people. Maybe this was how he liked to work.

She'd still been angry at Matheo's approach but finally agreed to his plan, because, as Nick said, he was an important client and they needed to establish a good working relationship with him. She pointed out to Nick that working closely with him was difficult, since they were meant to despise each other. But she conceded she'd enjoyed his company at dinner, especially after she was able to drop the bombshell about the Sandpiper into his life.

Now she thought back over the morning and decided she'd set the ground rules at breakfast. Matheo didn't know about the unreasonable panic that consumed her when she felt she was being backed into a corner with no means of escape, but she hoped he'd remember to consult her about any decisions affecting her life in future.

He knew how much she resented his ownership of what had been her home. She knew he'd bought it in an act of revenge against his father.

She would have preferred it if her family had remained his enemy, rather than his father. How awful it must be to be estranged from your only family member. It must make him very unhappy, she thought, although he hid it well. Internalising that sort of pain was not good for anyone, though.

To be that unhappy amidst the perfection of St Celeste must be brutal, as if nature was laughing at you.

But working with Matheo had been easy. They'd rerun her presentation and he'd stopped her with a question when he wanted more detail on something. He'd understood her explanations immediately, every time. In the darkness of the conference room, she'd been able to hear from the timbre of his voice whether he liked a suggestion, or not. Whether something interested him or didn't capture his imagination.

It felt as though they were uneasily in tune with one another, trying each other out, testing each other, in a quiet way.

She hadn't expected to find it so enjoyable, and she hadn't wanted it to end, so when they'd covered all the points relating to the Hideaway for the day and she had new ideas to work on she delayed returning to her suite by asking Matheo questions about the island.

He was passionate about his home, and keen to share that passion with her. He'd commissioned a young architect to design the buildings, with the idea of making them as eco-friendly as possible. Rainwater was harvested and stored in an underground cistern. Solar panels on the roofs generated electricity, which was stored in batteries in the basement. The gardens, planted with native species to withstand the hot summers and stormy winters, were irrigated by a natural spring, which rose in the centre of the island.

The timber for the soaring, curved shapes of the buildings was sourced from sustainable forests, and the glass was all recycled.

He admitted that the helicopter—and the private jet he also owned—were indulgent, but he often needed to travel at short notice. To compensate, in a small way, he made large donations to climate-change organisations each year.

Cassandra was awestruck by how he'd been able to translate his passion for protecting the environment into reality.

She felt herself adjusting her opinion of him, wondering how much more there was to discover about his ideas; about him. She could no longer think of him as simply the spoilt billionaire son of a billionaire father, forcing her to sell her home to him because of an age-old argument over a game of cards. With his considered opinions and concern for his surroundings, she wondered what had driven him to want to acquire the Hideaway in an act of revenge against his father. That behaviour felt out of character for the person who'd shown her a little more of himself through his enthusiasm for protecting this small island in the Mediterranean.

They'd eaten sandwiches at the conference table without interrupting their discussion. He hoped to use as many environmentally friendly features as possible in the renovated Hideaway, he said. For Cassandra, who'd imagined the hotel being pulled to bits by a developer with profit the only goal, this was almost unbelievable.

While the hotels that had made him famous, and rich, were all big names, in big cities across the globe, he wanted to move to smaller, boutique establishments, where he could implement his innovative ideas. The Hideaway was the first in what he hoped would be a chain of similar hotels, each incorporating sound eco principles but maintaining their original identities.

Cassandra reflected that only twenty-four hours earlier she'd thought the project was lost. She stretched her arms above her head and then began to re-read her notes. Her head was bursting with ideas.

Matheo had a business meeting and dinner in Nice in the late afternoon. A meal would be served in her suite and he'd see her for breakfast the following morning.

It was one in the morning before Matheo landed back on St Celeste. He wondered if the noise of the helicopter had woken Cassandra and whether he should knock on her door and suggest a night-cap.

He quickly decided that was a bad idea. She didn't like things being sprung on her—he'd learned that, and he wondered what had triggered that response. He wouldn't pry. It might send her into a panic and drive her away. Because he'd made it clear she could leave when she wished. He hadn't suggested she could also stay longer.

He pulled off his jacket and tie in his bedroom and slid open the door to his private terrace. The meeting and charity dinner this evening had been unavoidable. As one of the trustees he'd needed to show up, but the hours had dragged and he'd found himself constantly thinking how much more enjoyable dinner last night, on the terrace with Cassandra, had been. Their day today had essentially been one long business meeting, but it hadn't felt like work. It had all been pure pleasure.

CHAPTER ELEVEN

MATHEO LOOKED AT the screen but his brain wouldn't engage with it. He pressed the heels of his hands into his eyes and looked again, but his mind would not cooperate.

Not while her pale forearm lay so close to his bronzed one on the table, and her slim fingers flew over the keyboard, pulling up a screenful of images of cool interiors, warm Persian rugs and deep sofas. Her fragrant scent, of lavender and lemon, sifted over him, and he inhaled it despite knowing it would only disconnect his brain even more.

She'd be leaving tomorrow, and he could hardly bear the thought.

He'd become comfortable working with her. Their intellectual understanding seemed to run deep and he felt they were seamlessly connected in their goals for the Hideaway project. Nick had emailed sketches and Cassandra had skilfully translated them into three-dimensional images on her computer.

They'd spent hours, earlier in the day, back in

the darkened conference room, looking at them on the big screen, discussing the fall of light, the angle of a staircase, the necessity of each room having a view, whether of the sea, the garden or the wooded, rolling hills.

When he'd joked, two days ago, that there'd be no distractions in the darkened conference room, he'd been wrong.

He found her enthusiasm, her knowledge of her business, her interest in his ideas, just her *presence,* were major distractions. She was natural and relaxed and seemed unaware that when her arm had brushed against his in the dark a charge raced across his skin, spreading an awareness of her closeness through his whole body. He'd held himself rigid, avoiding touching her again, but desperately wanting to see what would happen if he did.

They agreed on almost everything, but she wasn't afraid to argue a point with him when she felt strongly about it. It was refreshing, when so many of the people he dealt with simply acquiesced as a matter of course. Wealth brought comfort and privilege, but it meant he never knew for sure if people wanted to be with him for *who* he was or for *what* he was. It made it impossible to have a meaningful discussion, a frank exchange of ideas. He got what he wanted but at the cost of never knowing whether another solution might have been better.

Beneath the table their knees had been inches apart. If he'd moved his chair to the left, just a fraction, they'd touch. He'd wanted to, but he didn't. What if she recoiled, shocked? What if she didn't?

It had been a relief when he could get up and restore the room to its normal brightness. Continuing their discussion in the light would be much easier.

Except it wasn't.

In the shade of the umbrella on the terrace, he found himself fascinated by the dancing colours in her eyes as she described something with enthusiasm or puzzled over an element of design. They held a Zoom meeting with Nick in London, to clarify points of the contract, and he had to concentrate, hard, on speaking to him and not being distracted by Cassandra's pure profile, the curve of her neck where it joined her shoulder, the shadow at the V-neck of her dress.

Perhaps it would have been sensible to cut her stay short. Probably he should never have suggested she stay at all. The rock on which he'd re-established himself two years ago felt unstable. He felt threatened by feelings he'd vowed he would never entertain again. If he allowed them to gain traction, he'd open himself to the possibility of pain and humiliation, all over again.

He believed in honesty and fairness, *integrity* above all else. But if Cassandra discovered the true man who lurked beneath the version he presented to the world, her beautiful eyes would fill with pity, and then derision.

He couldn't bear the thought of that, either.

She was fired up with a positivity he envied. Surely no-one could come within her orbit, in this mood, and not willingly be sucked into it. He angled the laptop away from his line of vision and rested his forearms on the table. The glass felt cool beneath his heated skin.

Surprise brought her thickly fringed eyes snapping up from the screen.

Matheo sucked in a breath and slid his gaze beyond her. The sea shone, blue and white, beneath the Mediterranean sky and the faint shape of a ship broke the perfect line of the horizon. When he looked at her again, she was watching him. He avoided eye contact and glanced down at the table.

'I think,' he said, quietly, 'that I—we—need a break. From all this. It's…a lot to absorb, in a short time.'

In the quiet that followed, Matheo was sharply aware of the distant mew of a seagull, wheeling over the waves, and the sad sighing of the breeze through the Stone pines that clothed the slopes of the island. These background sounds, he thought, would now remind him for ever of the time Cassandra Greenwood had invaded his personal space. It would always feel a little poorer, lonelier, for her absence.

He watched her chest rise on a deep breath. She shut down the computer and flipped the lid closed.

'A break?' Her brows contracted together. 'Are you saying you want me to leave? Because I'm leaving tomorrow. But if there's a flight, I could get it tonight, I could…'

'No. No, that's not what I'm saying. Unless you want to leave, of course… I wouldn't want to force you.'

'Force me to stay, or force me to leave?' He saw a flicker of uncertainty in her eyes, and in the way her teeth closed over her full lower lip.

'Neither, Cassandra. I know you don't like… that is, I know you like to make your own decisions, or at least discuss options.' He ran his hand over his jaw, wondering how he'd got into this discussion when all he'd wanted—*needed*—was the chance to try to get his reactions to her under control.

'How do you know that?' She picked up the pencil she'd been using earlier and tapped it on the glass tabletop. 'Has Nick said something?' Suspicion edged her voice.

'Nick? No, not at all. Besides, I promised you I wouldn't discuss anything that affects you, without your participation. Didn't I?'

She nodded. 'Yes. But that doesn't mean…'

'It means I wouldn't. I've told you before that I don't break promises.'

Cassandra folded her arms across her chest. He noticed the tips of her fingernails whiten with the pressure put on her upper arms. He remembered how his hands had circled them in that exact spot, and how fragile, yet strong, she'd felt.

Perhaps that was the essence of her. She was strong, forthright, determined, principled, but all those good traits hid a fragility which she was at pains to keep covered up.

'I want to believe you,' she said, 'but I don't find it easy.'

The breeze off the sea lifted the hem of her skirt and she smoothed it down, trapping it with both hands. A glossy lock of her hair, dark against the ivory skin of her cheek, whipped across her face and Matheo, without thinking, reached out and smoothed it away, tucking it behind her ear.

She tensed and moved away from him, and he dropped his hand.

'Has someone,' he asked gently, 'made it difficult for you to believe, in the past?'

She was silent for a beat. Then she nodded, once.

'Yes. He promised he'd… he said things would be better…if I did as he wanted, but…' She shook her head. 'I don't need…you don't need to know about it.'

'I think I'd like to, though. If you want to tell me.'

'It's over. I've dealt with it. But sometimes, when I'm feeling unsure about something, or unhappy, there're things I can't cope with. I panic if I feel trapped or threatened.'

'So the past year has been difficult for you. You were fighting a battle you must have known you couldn't win. You were on your own, with the weight of responsibility for the Hideaway staff on your shoulders. And then, when you'd made the most difficult decision of your life, possibly, I came along and forced you to make an even more difficult one. Is that about right?'

Cassandra nodded, biting her lip again, her eyes fixed on the sea below them.

'When my mother was ill, my father promised he'd make her better. He really believed he could do it if he tried hard enough. I don't think he was at all prepared when she died. I certainly wasn't. All I could think of was he'd promised, and the promise was broken.' She unfolded her arms and lifted the heavy skein of her hair off her neck, pulling the plait over her shoulder and twisting it in her hands. 'Then he seemed to pretend that she hadn't died at all. Everything had to be kept exactly as it was, as if he expected her to walk in the door at any moment. That was even more confusing.'

'I'm sure he didn't intend to make things worse for you. He was locked in grief from which he seemed to have no escape. I saw that for myself. Did he ever accept her loss, do you think?'

'No. I don't think he ever came close to acceptance. He was on medication for depression, but he needed more help than that. The only reason I managed to go away to college was because I knew the staff would care for him. They did, so you see why I owed them a debt. Then, in my first job, I met Jason. I was flattered by his attention. It was a relief to find someone who would care for me for a change. And he did, for a while.'

Matheo could see where this story was going and already felt angry. 'Only then you found his care came with a hefty price tag. Is that it?'

'Mmm. He was very good at withholding affection and approval unless I did as he demanded. I understand now that it was emotional blackmail and coercion, but when you're in the middle of something like that it's not easy to see, or accept, what it is.'

He clenched his fists and felt his jaw tighten, fury at the unknown man boiling through his veins. 'Bastard,' he grated.

Her quick glance was surprised. 'It's ok. I ended it. His fury when I refused to move in with him was off the scale and it made me afraid of him. Luckily, I got away. I had to change jobs because we worked for the same company, but that turned out to be a positive thing. I met Nick and we started FuturePlan, and…'

'And Nick?'

'Nick understands. He encouraged me to see a therapist. He knows what situations I find stressful and helps me to manage them positively, rather than by avoidance. Like staying here to work with you. I felt as if I had no control, that the decision had been made for me, by you, because it was what you wanted. Leaving would have been avoiding dealing with my reaction. Nick helped me to get it into proportion and to allow me to control my anxiety.'

Matheo drew in a long brcath. He'd been avoiding his next question for days, because he was afraid of her answer, but he knew he had to ask it now.

'Are you and Nick…partners on any other level? Is that why he understands you so well?'

'No.' She looked up at him. 'It's strictly business and friendship between us. Nick is married. To Dan. He's a lawyer.'

Matheo released the breath he hadn't realised he'd been holding and breathed out his tension. He hadn't wanted to ask about her relationship with Nick because he didn't want it to look as if he cared.

It seemed that he cared, a lot.

Cassandra dropped her bag, stripped off the linen dress and pulled on her bikini and silk kaftan. Then she headed out onto the veranda, grateful for the shade and for the cool sea breeze, which stirred in the muslin curtains behind her.

She sat on the top step and looked across the

beach to the sea. She should message Matheo now, before she could overthink this. She'd tell him she had to leave today.

But when she picked up her phone she remembered the expression in his eyes when he thought he was hiding it. He'd looked stricken when she'd suggested she could bring forward her departure and, in that instant, before he'd dropped his gaze, she'd glimpsed his loneliness.

They'd both lost people they'd loved. She had lost her parents and her home, and his mother had died and he was estranged from his father. The close, loving relationship she'd enjoyed with her parents meant she could not imagine the torment it must cause him, whatever the reasons behind it.

She'd navigated grief and despair with help from caring friends and her therapist, but Matheo had retreated to this island, where, except for his attentive staff, he was alone. He seemed to have no support network.

But she couldn't allow sympathy to colour her judgement. She'd worked hard to shed the negative influences of her toxic relationship with Jason. She mostly felt comfortable with how she coped with the world.

She was in danger of jeopardising that.

Being near Matheo was becoming increasingly difficult. She reminded herself, repeatedly, that he was a Chevalier and therefore never to be trusted, but that thread, which had first tugged them towards each other fourteen years ago, still stretched between them, pulling at her each time they met. She was sure he felt it, too.

In the darkened conference room, she'd experienced a moment of madness when she longed for him to touch her, to make her feel cherished and special. To have him show he cared for her, just for a minute. She'd stood firmly on her own feet for so long, steering clear of any emotional involvement or physical contact with anyone else, and sometimes it became exhausting.

She'd shoved her treacherous feelings aside and leaned away from him, putting a few more inches of physical distance between them. He was the most important client they'd ever had. He was the billionaire every company hoped to attract. Somehow, she and Nick had caught a lucky star, and she felt as if she was about to destroy it.

Because anything apart from a strict business relationship between them would be a disaster, professionally and personally. Mixing business and pleasure never worked.

They'd signed the contract and so she had made up her mind to trust him on a professional level. Trusting him on a personal level, with her emotions, was a different thing altogether.

He bore a destructive grudge against his father, which he refused to discuss. How could she ever trust someone who wished their own father ill?

Never, was the answer. This was reckless physical desire, nothing more. It came from spending too much time together, in a romantic and exotic location, finding qualities in each other they'd each thought the other lacked, and discovering a shared passion for beauty and sustainability in the built and natural environment.

But none of these logical arguments could stop her from feeling herself light up each time she saw him. Neither could they take away the longing to experience the brush of his lips on her cheek again, or his steady hands on her arms, holding her upright in the cold sea.

All this meant she really should leave this evening, even if she had to spend the night at a hotel at Nice Airport. She'd be safe there, from Matheo and, most of all, from herself.

He'd suggested meeting again at five o'clock. She'd tell him then that she had to leave.

At a minute to five Cassandra came walking towards him where he waited at the foot of the steps. She stopped and he saw a flash of confusion cross her features before her gaze narrowed. Both her hands curled around the strap of her satchel.

'What's happening, Matheo?' Her eyes travelled over him. 'I thought we were having a meeting.'

He glanced down at his board shorts and bare feet. 'We're not having a meeting. We're having a picnic.'

CHAPTER TWELVE

ALLOWING HIM TO bring her to this secluded place had been all kinds of foolish. But he'd looked so relaxed—and *pleased*—when he'd announced the picnic she hadn't wanted to refuse. Most of all, she hadn't been able to say what she should have said. The faint lines of anxiety, an almost permanent fixture on the handsome planes of his face, had softened with his smile. Turning down the invitation to accompany him would have felt childish. Telling him she wanted to return to the mainland, to spend the night in an airport hotel, would have felt massively ungrateful.

But now she regretted the way she'd followed him through the trees to the jetty without a murmur.

At the end of the beach, smooth boulders tumbled haphazardly into the turquoise water. The tide, slight as it was in the Mediterranean, must be coming in because the line of her footprints, pressed into the pristine sand, were already blurred by the push and pull of rippling water.

Slanting sunlight feathered through the branches of the tall pines that fringed the cove.

The sleek silver and white boat bobbed in the shallow water, its anchor rope slack. They had skimmed over the glassy sea, the wind in their faces, until Matheo had throttled back the engine and spun the wheel, turning in to where this crescent of sand curved between two headlands. She could see he'd spread out a rug and carried a picnic basket ashore. She heard the muted pop of a champagne cork.

'What are we celebrating?' she called as she made her way back towards him.

He handed her a flute of fizz and gestured to their surroundings. 'Let's just settle for being here.' He took a mouthful of champagne. 'Do you like it?'

She nodded, sipping from her glass. 'It's… beautiful, yes. Remote.'

'It's my favourite place on the island. Probably in the world. It's where I find true peace and quiet.'

'And solitude?'

'That too.' His brows drew together. 'Do you have a favourite place?'

Cassandra bit her lip, unwilling to spoil the moment.

'Do you need to ask?'

His frown deepened. 'I'm sorry. That was a thoughtless question.'

'Yes, perhaps.' She shrugged. 'But over the

past few days, working with you, it's begun to feel less...*raw*. It helps, knowing I have a say in how it's going to be and knowing how closely your ideas match my own. In an odd way it feels as if I'm preparing the Hideaway for the future, a new lease of life, rather than losing it.'

'I'm glad. That makes me feel less guilty for being the one to take your home from you.'

She sat down, her legs folded under her. 'I've been working all day...'

'You've been working all week. I decided it was time for a break.'

'*You* decided, huh?'

She saw the implication of her words register, and she smiled.

'I'm sorry. I should have checked with you first...are you teasing me?'

'Just a little. I'm happy to take a break. And I love picnics.'

'I also wanted to show you more of St Celeste. You can't leave tomorrow without seeing some of it.'

They ate tiny, juicy tomatoes dipped in humous, and spicy sliced salami. There was French bread to soak up fruity olive oil and salty olives stuffed with almonds. The chef had sliced ripe peaches into a dish of raspberry coulis, and as Cassandra licked peach juice off her fingers she rolled her eyes.

'Delicious.' She held out the bowl for him. 'Have some.'

Matheo removed his shades and his iron-dark eyes fixed on her mouth. Her heart lurched as he reached towards her, but he was offering her a paper napkin.

'You have juice on your chin.'

His voice was as smooth and dark as good chocolate. The brush of his fingers as she took the napkin sent a shiver rippling through her.

This was why she should have left.

Her defences against this pull between them, which grew tighter and more intense each time they met, were crumbling. It was wrong and unfaithful of her to feel this way. Matheo and his family stood for everything her father and her ancestors had fought against and loathed, and to betray them was unthinkable. And her determined belief in her own strength and resilience could be shattered.

She shuffled a little further away from him, out of his reach.

'Tell me more about the island. Has it belonged to your family for decades?'

Matheo drained his glass and tucked it into the basket. He rested his elbows on his bent knees and looked beyond Cassandra towards the sea. His eyes, hard as flint, had lost their smile.

'The island,' he said, 'does not belong to my family. It belongs to me. I bought it. I developed the buildings. I decide who visits.' His implacable gaze shifted and connected with hers. 'And the guestlist no longer includes my family. Not ever.'

The tension radiating from him made the air between them snap.

'Ah, so that's an awkward subject,' she ventured. 'You've mentioned the rift…'

She'd never heard a laugh more dry or devoid of humour. She wanted to reach out to him; to somehow dispel the anger and stress in his tense muscles, to soften his rigid mouth, bring that warm flame of emotion back into his eyes, but she felt afraid of what her touch might unleash. 'Matheo…'

He stopped her with a quick shake of his head. 'A rift.' He seemed to taste the word to try it out. 'That's a…tidy…word for the explosion that ripped my life apart.' He pulled a hand across his face.

Silence stretched between them, marked by the rhythmic wash and suck of the sea and the sudden, restless shushing of a sunset breeze in the trees.

She picked up the spoon with which she'd eaten the peaches and rubbed a thumb over the smooth silver handle. Its curve was a comforting shape.

'Do you want to tell me why you've gone to such insane lengths to settle a score with your father? Because I don't understand how…'

'Of course you don't understand.' His hands

were bunched into fists, his knuckles gleaming white beneath the stretched skin. 'How could you?'

'I thought you'd bought the Hideaway on behalf of your father. I hope, now that you've thwarted his plans to own it, you feel better. Perhaps you'll be able to let go.'

He glanced across at her, shaking his head.

'I thought it would make me feel better too, but it hasn't. My father…betrayed me…and nothing I can do is going to repair the damage. There's nothing he can do, either. Not any more.'

'Do you want to tell me about it?'

'I've told you before, it's a personal matter. I do not discuss it.'

Cassandra's heart fell as she realised he was not going to break the silence that held his pain captive. His expression had closed down. The iron-cold remoteness of his eyes told her she was pushing against a wall which would never give way. She tried one last tactic.

'Is it,' she asked softly, 'about your mother?'

The breeze ruffled across the water and she shivered, wrapping her arms around herself.

'You're cold. We should head back.' He reached into the bag and pulled out a beach towel. 'I brought these in case we went for a swim.'

'Thank you. And I'm sorry I asked about your mother.'

He shook his head, flicking his hair off his forehead.

'That's okay. It's not about her, although, looking back, my father's treatment of her was enough to cause me to hate him. At the time I was too young to realise.'

Cassandra pulled the towel around her shoulders, tucking up her knees and feet. 'What happened, Matheo?'

'Her illness was kept quiet. I was shocked and completely unprepared for her death. Rather like you.'

'No.' Cassandra shook her head. 'I knew my mother was ill. I just believed she'd get better.'

'I was sent to boarding school the week after she died. Crying was considered babyish, and grief was seen as self-pity. I learned to bury my emotions and I learned to defend myself against the bullying. Eventually I was expelled, for breaking one nose too many.' He smiled. 'I considered that achievement to be the greatest of my school career. Obviously, I was sent to another school, but my reputation preceded me and I was left alone. I was a little disappointed. I had so much anger to get rid of.'

'So you've never had any help, dealing with the loss of your mother?'

'None. It was as if she simply hadn't existed. A few years ago, I managed to find out where she was buried but I'd never been able to face visiting her grave. Not until a couple of weeks ago.'

Cassandra thought back to where he would have been.

'Was that after you left Cornwall?'

He nodded. 'I was on my way back here. It was our meeting in the churchyard that prompted me. I've arranged for her grave to be properly tended now.'

Cassandra wanted to put her arms around him to comfort him, but she stayed wrapped in the towel a safe distance away.

'That is such an important and special thing to have done,' she whispered. 'You must feel good about it.'

'Yes, surprisingly, I do. Would you… I thought about doing the same for your parents, but I knew I should ask you first, if I saw you again.'

There was a long silence while Cassandra considered his offer; thought about the kindness behind the suggestion. Then she shook her head.

'That is one of the kindest offers I've had for a long time, but at the moment… I'll need to think about it for a bit. With our history…it might feel inappropriate.'

'Of course. I understand. But if you should change your mind, let me know.' He stood up in a supple movement, holding out a hand towards her. 'We should be getting back. We'll catch the last of the sunset from the water if we hurry.'

Cassandra accepted his hand and he pulled her to her feet. Their shoulders collided and he moved away but kept her hand gripped in his.

'Come on. I'll take you to the boat. We don't want you falling over in the sea.'

Matheo leaned against the balustrade, swirling amber whisky in a heavy glass tumbler. He'd been for a run, trying in vain to dispel some of his pent-up frustration. A cold shower afterwards hadn't helped, either. His board shorts and T-shirt clung to his damp skin because he'd been too agitated to dry himself properly. He'd resorted to a bottle of his favourite malt, hoping a measure of the smoky spirit would calm him.

Images of Cassandra were running on a loop in his brain and it was driving him insane.

He'd come close, so terrifyingly close, to cracking and telling her what his father had done. Just thinking about it made him feel vulnerable and small. He'd never talk about it. He'd made that decision two years ago. If he did, he'd hand the control of it to someone else. As long as he kept it screwed down tight, he'd have it under control himself.

Cassandra made him softer. He could feel some of the tension he held in his body melt away every time he came close to her. It wasn't just her calming scent; that was tantalising enough. It was her aura of kindness and concern for others, her sympathetic, deep blue eyes, her sparkling enthusiasm for the work she did which entranced him. She should hate him, but she'd been able to turn those negative emotions into a positive vision for the future. She should resent her father and the failing business he'd bequeathed her, but she didn't, making allowances for him instead, and spending her trust fund on paying the staff. He wished he could allow himself to absorb just a fraction of her open-hearted, warm spirit.

Surely he'd feel less bitter if he could. But what if that bitterness had become so much a part of him that he could never shake it off? Buying the Hideaway had not given him the resolution he'd expected. What if he always felt there was another score to settle with his father?

It was a bleak thought.

He pushed himself upright and turned, intending to top up his drink, but a movement on the beach caught his eye. He looked again. Cassandra was walking across the sand towards the seashore. Under the moon, the scene was a monochrome study in silver and black, and her limbs glowed pale in the unearthly light. She'd released her hair to let it flow around her face and down her back in a shimmering black mass, and she'd replaced the linen dress with the silk top she'd worn last night. It blew softly around her thighs, catching points of moonshine as she moved. She was gaining speed with every step.

Matheo watched, fascinated, memory tugging at his consciousness. As she reached the point where the ripples of water spent themselves into nothing on the sand, she pulled the top over her head. He thought she was wearing a bikini but it might have been underwear. She spread her arms wide and turned in a circle and threw back her head. Then she began to dance in and out of the shallow water, her feet skipping over the little foam-crested waves, twirling and dipping in a rhythm of her own making. He'd defy anyone who didn't know better not to believe they were seeing some ethereal sea nymph emerging from the water to dance for the sea gods.

And then the jagged pieces of memory that were rattling around in his brain started to fall, one at a time, into place. He was twenty-five again and back on a beach in Cornwall. He'd walked away from the furious argument raging between his father and Joe Greenwood and found his way to the beach. He was supposed to be backing his father up, providing the supporting arguments to his bid for the hotel, but he'd had no stomach for it.

Raw grief had permeated every corner of the place, and a kind of desperation informed every word Joe spoke—or, rather, shouted. Matheo had been stopped in his tracks by the sheer, unfathomable depth of sorrow that gaped in front of him whichever way he turned. He'd wondered how the loss of a single life could cause such an explosion of despair. He'd tried in vain to persuade his father to give up, go away, and leave these people to their overwhelming sadness.

The girl, who'd been a footnote to the few days they'd spent there, was on the beach.

He'd struck up a tenuous connection with her, once she'd realised he meant no harm and did not want to talk about the Hideaway. He'd had the feeling she hadn't talked to anyone else for weeks. She embodied his idea of a sprite, quick and elusive, disappearing among the rocks if he asked the wrong question or got too close.

He'd stood very still and watched as she danced in and out of the waves, lifting her skirt clear of the water, her long bare legs flashing in the low afternoon sun. Her hair blew out behind her in a tangled mass of curls, which looked as if they hadn't seen a brush or comb for weeks. For the first time in days, Matheo had felt a lifting of the gloom that sat, heavy as a storm cloud, over the hunched old building on the hill above them. He'd stepped forward and called her name.

She'd stopped, head turned towards him, standing stock still, and he remembered, suddenly and vividly, how the next wave had washed around her calves, catching the drooping hem of her skirt. And then she'd gathered it and taken to her heels, running like a deer through the shallow water towards the rocks at the far end of the beach. But the wet fabric had tangled around her legs, and she'd tripped…

By the time he'd reached her she was stumbling to her knees, pushing her hair out of her eyes.

'Let me help you… I'm sorry I surprised you. You don't need to be afraid.' He'd lifted her out of the shallow water, his hands around her upper arms, holding her as gently as he could. 'It's okay. I won't hurt you.' Instinctively, he'd spoken softly, anxious not to scare her.

She'd swayed towards him as she tried to regain her balance and looked up at him. He was captivated by her eyes, fringed with thick dark lashes, and her full lower lip, and for a fleeting second he'd thought he was going to kiss her. He'd dropped his head and slid one hand to the small of her back, knowing it was wrong but not knowing if he could resist her. He'd felt her stiffen and then she broke away from him and ran.

'No! Wait!' he'd called, but he might as well have been calling the wind. She'd reached the end of the beach and scrambled over the rocks, which the cliff had scattered into the sea, and by the time he got to them there was no trace of her. She'd vanished into thin air.

And then, just a few weeks ago, she'd slithered down that stepladder, into his arms. But he'd known all along that beneath the business reasons for his visit to the Hideaway had been the hope that she'd be there.

Now here she was, dancing on *his* beach this time. She was grown up, successful and self-confident but still wild when she allowed herself to be. He was through the door and halfway down the stairs before he realised what he was doing.

Cass shivered as the water swirled around her ankles, but she soon forgot its chill as sheer exhilaration seized her. How long was it since she'd danced on the beach? She couldn't remember, but the release it brought her was as clear in her mind as if it were yesterday. It had started when she was a baby. Her mother had danced in and out of the waves with Cass in her arms, and it had continued ever since. It was the best stress-buster she knew, and the best way to forget the bad times and revel in the good ones, however meagre they seemed.

She lost all track of time but eventually she paused, breathless, with the waves washing around her knees, and then she sank down into the silky water. She rolled onto her back and gazed up at the night sky.

She'd needed this, to break the tension that had thrummed through her ever since Matheo had taken her hand on the beach. The desire to turn into him, against his wide chest, to wrap them both in the towel he'd given her and just be with him, skin to skin, for a few seconds had been powerful. Resisting it had taken huge determination and she'd had to find a way to reset herself.

The sea had always been her place of solace and it had done its work.

She felt cleansed and refreshed as she picked her way back across the beach. The night breeze raised goose-bumps on her wet skin as she mounted the shallow steps onto the terrace.

A shadow detached itself from the darkness by the wall. She stopped, panting slightly, an arm's length from where Matheo stood. She was ready for anything.

Anything but this.

Silence, taut as a bowstring, stretched between them. He broke it first. 'Are you alright?'

'I'm fine. Thank you.'

It sounded abrupt but it was the truth.

'You must be a little cold. I brought a towel.'

He stepped forward and dropped a warm towel around her shoulders.

'Have you been watching me?'

'I have.'

'Why?'

She clutched the towel at her neck, wanting very much to get past him.

'I saw you from the terrace. It reminded me of seeing you dance on the beach in Cornwall.'

'Really?' She laughed. 'That's a bit unlikely.'

'Not recently. Years ago. When my father and I were there.'

Cass stiffened.

The memory, which had been flitting in and out of her brain for the past few weeks, suddenly became more tangible. Running down the beach, away from him. Tripping in the water. The feel of his hands on her arms, and that overwhelming desire to sink against him. To let him carry her burdens. Hearing her name called on the wind, but keeping on running…

'Oh!' she exclaimed, exhaling sharply. '*That* time.'

He moved aside so she could cross the threshold and followed her, putting his hand out to flick the light switch.

'I'm going to have a shower. I need to warm up. You can go, now you know I'm okay.'

Her throat felt tight and narrow and forming the words was a strain.

'I'll wait.'

'What for?'

She was avoiding his eyes, but that meant she was looking at the rest of him, and not finding any bit of him wanting. The neck of his T-shirt revealed tanned skin stretching over the tips of his collarbones, and she wanted, urgently, to bury her face there and breathe him in.

Finally, unavoidably, their eyes collided and the shock of what she saw in his made her try to step back. He felt the chemistry fizzing between them. He knew she felt it too and he was as out of control of it as she was. She swayed slightly, off balance, and felt his hand on her shoulder, steadying her.

'I need to apologise. I spoke harshly earlier.'

'What?' Her voice caught in her impeded throat, surprise blurring her reason. 'I thought you never made mistakes.'

'I don't know where you got that idea. I've made plenty, and at least one of them has been… catastrophic.'

'Matheo, I'm not comfortable with this.'

'Let me help you, then.'

'I didn't mean the towel.'

But his other hand had come up to where she was clutching the towel and was peeling her fingers away from it. It slipped to the floor, leaving her in the soaked bikini, which stuck to her body in dark wetness. She shivered as he slid a hand around the back of her head, tangling his fingers in her hair and pulling her towards him.

She knew she shouldn't, but she wanted this, more than she ever remembered wanting anything. She was drowning in the black depths of his eyes, losing all sense of time and space as his other hand came up to trap hers against him.

'I shouldn't want this…'

'Why not?'

'Do we even *like* each other?'

The first light, sure touch of his lips silenced her. Then he lifted his head and pulled her in, running his hands down her back, over her bottom. He pressed her pliancy against the rigidity of his body, bracing her against his rock-hard thighs and easing her head back to expose her throat. She felt his cool, dry lips touch the place there where her pulse beat, and then trace a path upwards to claim her mouth again.

This time there was no question of holding back. As his tongue parted the seam of her lips and invaded her mouth any resistance melted into a pool of pure, unfamiliar desire. Her arms went around his neck, pulling him down to deepen the kiss, kissing him back with a desperation bordering on insanity. Her body leapt in response as his hands travelled over her, and she pushed her own hands beneath his shirt, revelling in the feel of the hot silk of his skin shivering under her touch.

He was demolishing her defences and she was letting him do it, telling herself it was just this once. He made her body sing and her mind reel but tomorrow she'd leave and return to real life, where billionaire clients did not desire women like her, with control hang-ups and wild urges to dance in the sea.

She took a ragged breath as he gently nipped her bottom lip and then ran his tongue down her neck to the acutely sensitive hollow of her shoulder, and then she groaned in protest as he raised his head and rested his cheek against her hair, trapping her hands in his to stop their exquisite exploration of his body.

'I'm sorry. I didn't mean this to happen.'

Finally, her breathing quick and shallow, she got to bury her face in his chest and absorb the scent of him. She filled her lungs with it, concentrating hard, determined to remember it, because she knew this was never going to happen again. She felt his strong, capable hands smoothing her hair, caressing her back, and thought shakily that he didn't need to apologise for making her feel so amazing.

'Two apologies, Matheo, in quick succession,' she heard herself saying. 'But it's all right. I'm okay. I wanted this, very much.'

She was far from okay, because she wanted to stay here, in the circle of his arms, for ever, to kiss him again and to see what would happen after that. If he would hold her and help to satisfy the ache of longing which had started up in her heart, nothing else mattered. She shook her head against him, her lips brushing his skin, and she felt his abrupt intake of breath. Then he put firm hands on her shoulders and forced a small gap between them. 'Your shirt's wet,' she said shakily, glancing down.

'Small price.'

He wrapped his arms around her again and touched his forehead to hers.

'Cassandra?'

'Mmm…?'

'Stay.'

Her eyes, which had drifted closed, flew open.

'What?'

'Stay. Here with me, on St Celeste. We work well together, and we could explore…this thing between us. I think you've known for as long as I have that it exists.'

She nodded slowly, her eyes fixed on his.

'Yes. It exists. But we don't have to give in to it. It—this—feels amazing, but… I can't stay, Matheo.' She dropped her head onto his shoulder, inhaling his clean, soapy scent. 'I was going to tell you I wanted to leave this afternoon, but then you'd organised the picnic. I needed to go, to protect myself, and now I think I should have. But I wanted to be with you too.'

He shifted his stance, pulling her closer.

'Protect yourself from me? Cassandra, I'd never hurt you, or make you do anything you don't want.'

'Mostly from myself. Because I want you but I have to go back to London soon. And what would happen then? Perhaps you'd be okay with a no-strings fling, but I can't do that. I've worked hard to make myself strong, and I can't risk it.'

'Do you think you'll ever feel strong enough?'

'I don't think I'll know unless I meet someone who makes me feel…safe, through trust.'

'How do I make you feel?'

'Excited, crazy…impulsive, inspired. All dangerous.'

He put his hands on her shoulders and eased her further away from him.

'I'm glad you didn't leave this afternoon because then we wouldn't have had this.' He dropped a kiss on her hair. 'You're right about me. I'm not the person you should trust with your emotions. But I think spending time with you has made me a better person. Less bad, anyway.'

Cassandra shook her head. 'No, Matheo. You're not bad. Don't think that of yourself. You had a traumatic childhood and something terrible has happened between you and your father…'

'Not that different from you, but you're positive, caring and warm. Everyone loves you.'

He turned her towards the bathroom door.

'You're shivering. Go and get warmed up.'

Cassandra stripped off her bikini and stood under the shower, turning the heat up as high as she could bear and staying until her teeth stopped chattering and she'd stopped shivering.

He was gone when she came out of the bathroom. She dried her hair roughly and climbed into bed, but she knew she could give up on sleep before she'd even tried. She was wired up and stressed and her body was in crazy overdrive, demanding something which she couldn't deliver. If this was desire, it was dangerous as hell. No wonder lust was a deadly sin.

CHAPTER THIRTEEN

'I DON'T AGREE with you, Nick.' Cassandra watched Nick twirl a pencil through his fingers in a complicated series of moves. 'And is that pencil actually an extension of your hand?'

Nick smiled. 'Don't change the subject. It won't work with me. It's rare that we don't agree on something, but this time I'm going to insist that I'm right.'

'But I got the trip to St Celeste. I lived in a bubble of luxury for five days—a whole working week. It's your turn. You should be the one to go to the conference.'

'Yes, a whole working week, and judging by the times at which some of your emails dropped into my inbox, you worked many more hours than in a normal week.'

Cass flicked her gaze away from his. 'Yes, we… I…did. But it didn't feel like work, in such a beautiful place, and Matheo and I…'

Nick waited. She wished she hadn't mentioned Matheo by name. She'd been careful to do that as little as possible, referring to him as 'Mr Chevalier' or 'the client'. Nick would have noticed that. And now he'd notice the silence. She rushed to fill it.

'We connected, on a professional level. It was easier than I thought it would be.'

'Good, because I did worry about you travelling out there on your own, to deal with such an established adversary. It's good you managed to put your differences aside and make progress on the project.' He tapped the end of the pencil on the table. 'The groundwork you did has been invaluable. Even if it apparently exhausted you.'

Cassandra opened her mouth to protest, but he held up a hand.

'You've looked tired and stressed ever since you returned...how many weeks ago? And you've lost weight.'

'That's from all the manual labour I did at the Hideaway. Who knew polishing floors and nailing slates onto a roof in a force-eight gale was such good exercise?'

'So I think you deserve a break. The conference in Dubai will be a blast. Have you been there?'

'No, but...'

'Well, then, that's decided. You need to see some of the incredible architecture, and there are interiors which defy description. You have to be there.'

'The Hideaway project—'

'Is going well. We're on schedule and there's no reason why you can't be away for a few days. You'll need to promote the company, at the exhibition, using the Sandpiper as an example of our latest success. And there's a gala reception, which will be a brilliant opportunity to meet people from across the globe and spread the message about FuturePlan.' He sent her a 'no arguments' look. 'And have some fun while you're there. Play the tourist. There's loads to see.'

Cassandra stood at the floor-to-ceiling window of her luxury room in one of the tallest hotels in the world and snapped a picture of the view on her phone. She sent it to Nick and added 'Thank you!' She knew he'd get the message she was trying to send.

She felt truly grateful to him for insisting she take this opportunity. The vibrancy and colour of the city and culture were so utterly different from Cornwall, London and, she dared herself to think, St Celeste that she'd been shaken out of herself by a host of new experiences. In between the morning and evening sessions at the exhibition centre, she'd braved the heat, still intense in September, and followed Nick's advice, and the previous two days had passed in a blur.

She'd been on a helicopter tour of the city and ridden a camel in the desert. She'd eaten dates and drunk thick, sweet coffee in a cavernous traditional tent, and raced over dunes and through wadis in a convoy of rugged four-by-four vehicles.

She'd chugged across the creek on an *abbra*, a traditional water taxi, past wharfs lined with dhows being loaded in preparation for voyages across the Arabian Sea. The labyrinth of lamplit alleys, which made up the old souk, had drawn her in with its scuffing of sandalled feet, and glimpses of bright silks worn by the women beneath their traditional black abayas.

The aroma of every spice in the world rose tantalisingly from the bags of vibrant powders and bunches of dried leaves and flowers, bringing to her a sudden sharp longing for India. The gold souk, with its wall-to-wall displays of intricate, bright jewellery and ropes of gleaming pearls, had left her speechless.

The heady scents of frankincense and myrrh still seemed to swirl about her as she tried to pull her attention back to where she stood.

She felt alive and carefree, for the first time for as long as she could remember, and she was looking forward to the gala reception in a few hours' time.

Nick pinged back a smiley face and a thumbs-up and she retreated to the bathroom to get ready.

The dress had been a perfect fit when she'd fallen in love with the lilacshot-silk fabric and bought it to wear to a charity ball a couple of years before. It was a little loose now, she thought, admitting that Nick was right about her weight loss. But the sculpted bodice still shaped her curves as the skirt flared over her hips and down to the floor in a shimmering sweep. She twisted to see the back and suddenly hoped it wasn't too daringly low.

'Too late,' she muttered. She had nothing else suitable. She clipped her amethyst pendant, inherited from her grandmother, around her neck and made sure the little sparkly clips that held her hair in place were secure. Then she threw an intricately embroidered shawl, which she'd bought in the souk, around her shoulders.

Outside her room, the passage curved towards the bank of lifts, the view down into the vast atrium unfolding as she walked. She was looking down at the throng of glamorous guests parading across the marble floor, far below, when the lift pinged behind her.

'Mon Dieu!'

She swung round, startled eyes flying wide at the achingly familiar, deep voice.

'Matheo...?' His name came out in a whisper, forcing itself past her constricted throat, shock and panic instantly racing through her, pumping adrenaline into her veins. She stood, frozen, unmoving, transfixed by his deep eyes, grey as a stormy sea.

The lift doors began to slide but he put out a

hand to keep them open. Then, with the other hand, he reached for her, cupped her elbow, and drew her into the space beside him.

The doors closed on a soft, vacuum sigh.

Matheo seemed to fill the space. His dinner jacket fitted so well, so *perfectly*, across those powerful shoulders and biceps. A black silk bow tie contrasted with the dazzling white of his cotton shirtfront, and a black satin cummerbund defined rather than disguised a washboard abdomen. She stared at him, her brain frozen, as the lift began its descent.

Matheo dropped his hand and stepped back. Shock made him doubt he was seeing correctly. Had his incessant thoughts of Cassandra finally tricked his mind into conjuring her up in front of him? When the doors opened and he stepped out into the ballroom, would she fade away into the ether, leaving her tantalising scent lingering on the warm air?

But she was breathing, quick and shallow, as colour suffused cheeks which at first had faded to a deathly pale.

He kept his distance. He couldn't trust himself to touch her again, even though he wanted to make sure she was not a figment of his overactive imagination. He looked past her, only to be met with the dozens of images of her cool radiance reflected in the mirrored walls. He cursed inwardly. Whose appalling idea had it been to fit lifts with mirrors?

'Cassandra?' He had barely allowed himself to think her name, let alone say it out loud, since he'd guided her, shivering in her wet bikini, into the bathroom on St Celeste and closed the door behind her. The word sounded alien to him. '*Cass?* How…? What are you doing here?'

'I…'

Her throat moved convulsively as she tried to speak and he saw the sparkle of an amethyst lying against her alabaster skin.

'Of course,' he said, 'an amethyst is the perfect jewel for you.'

'Thank you.' She nodded. 'I'm promoting the Sandpiper.'

What banal conversation, he thought, aware that the lift was sinking steadily, the numbers above the door counting down. He wanted it to stop. He had the insane thought that there might be a 'pause' button he could press, so he could be with her, alone, long enough to say something meaningful rather than comment stupidly on her jewellery.

But he remembered how she might react to that. She might panic, feel trapped in a situation over which she had no control. He'd never do that to her. He wanted her to trust him.

'I arrived a few hours ago,' he said. 'It's the one conference I force myself to attend. I come for the networking at the gala and meetings over the next few days.'

She nodded, adjusting the shawl she had wrapped around her shoulders. He longed to see beyond it. Did her gown cover her shoulders? She looked thinner. He could see a more pronounced hollow than he remembered where her skin stretched over her delicate collarbones.

'How…how have you been?' He meant so much more than that. Did she think of him the way he thought of her? In other words, most of the time? Had she missed their easy exchange of ideas about buildings, interiors and every other subject under the Mediterranean sun? Had she been back to Cornwall, stood ankle-deep in the freezing sea and wondered where he was; what he was doing?

'Okay, thank you. The Hideaway project is going very well. It should open in time for Christmas.'

He didn't need to be told about the Hideaway. He kept track of that, minutely following every detail of the development, looking for signs of Cassandra, of her name, anywhere, of hints of things they'd discussed, decided, on St Celeste.

'Good,' was all he could conjure up as the lift came quietly to a stop and the doors opened.

Matheo stepped out and into a surging press of the global hotel trade's most glamorous and wealthy operators. This was why, he thought, he hated these occasions, but this time he had one good reason to be here. He paused to cast a glance over the glittering crowd surging through the marble and gold ballroom.

A step behind him he felt Cassandra hesitate.

She wouldn't like this, he realised. The noise, the hard, reflective surfaces, the lights, all contributed to an atmosphere that felt as if it teetered on the brink of chaos. He couldn't imagine anything further from the kind of ambience he knew she favoured. From working with her he'd learned to appreciate her love of deep, luxurious fabrics and rugs, the arrangement of furniture and placement of objects, which all contributed to the establishment of a calm, relaxed vibe, whether it was in a private study or a public reception room.

He glanced over his shoulder and saw her stop, her eyes wide and anxious, her hands tightening on the edges of her shawl. He took half a step back and turned slightly towards her.

'Will you be alright? If we move through this crowd there'll be more space, and I'll ask for the doors to the terrace to be opened if you like. You might be more comfortable out there.'

She nodded, her teeth nipping her bottom lip, but she didn't move. A few curious glances came their way. A photographer, obviously employed to document the event, snapped their picture. Matheo thought Cassandra was seconds from turning and fleeing back into the lift and he didn't want that. He wanted her by his side.

Trying to make the gesture as natural and casual as possible, he slipped an arm around her waist and gently urged her closer to him.

He couldn't have predicted that beneath the silky fall of the embroidered shawl he would find the naked skin of her back. His heart missed a beat.

Satiny skin shivered under the tips of his fingers. Just how low was the cut of her gown? he wondered, but he didn't explore to find out. He tried to control the hot spike of desire, which threatened to make him do or say something unacceptable. Her anxiety levels were already sky-high. A wrong move from him would definitely send her into retreat. He tightened his arm and bent to reassure her, desperate to keep her with him.

'You can do this, Cassandra. I promise I'll take care of you.'

She looked up at him and the anxiety faded from her ink-blue eyes. She nodded.

'I'm sorry. This crowd took me by surprise. I'll be okay now.'

As Matheo reluctantly dropped his hand from her back, she linked her fingers through his and they moved forward.

He felt her relax a little as they wove their way through the press of guests to a less crowded part of the vast room. Her grip on his fingers loosened and she slowed her pace, glancing round instead of keeping her gaze fixed on the floor. He was glad she'd regained her equilibrium. With a quick, light pressure on her fingers, he eased his hand from hers. He smiled down at her. 'Feeling better?' he murmured.

She gave a nod as he took two glasses of champagne from a passing waiter.

'Here's to our chance meeting.' He clinked his glass against hers and their eyes locked.

'Thank you for rescuing me, Matheo. I could have easily backed out and returned to my room.'

He inclined his head towards her.

'I could feel that, but it would be a pity to miss out on this gathering. If you want…'

He saw her face light up with the smile he wished was reserved only for him and she put her fingers on his jacket sleeve.

'Excuse me, Matheo. I've just spotted an acquaintance. I must say hello.'

She turned with a swish of silk and he watched her thread her way through the crowd. Groups of people had spilled out onto the terrace, enjoying the warm evening, but the level of noise hadn't lessened. Keeping his back to the wall, he tried to keep an eye on Cassandra.

Time dragged. Matheo made small talk with a few people he knew and many he didn't. Glancing at his watch, he wondered how soon he could leave without appearing rude. His eyes roved over the assembled glitterati. Cassandra was unknown in this crowd, and he saw the curiosity that her unselfconscious beauty provoked in both men and women. She was engaged in animated conversation with a world-renowned hotelier. The man was a notorious womaniser and Matheo's fingers tightened around the stem of his champagne flute. If he so much as touched her…

'Matheo. What a surprise! We weren't expecting to see you here.'

The huskiness of the voice had the cultivated falseness he remembered. He raised his head and met the appraising stare of his stepmother. It was difficult to think of her in those terms. She was the same age as him, for God's sake. The advantage of surprise brought a glitter of triumph to her eyes as her fingers closed around his forearm. He took in her tanned face and ice-blonde hair and her thin frame. Then he looked beyond her, searching for his father.

'Charles is somewhere here,' she said, with a flick of her head. 'Talking business, as usual.'

'Claudia.' To his surprise his voice sounded perfectly normal. 'That is to be expected at an industry event.' He wished she'd remove her hand from his arm. He felt a pressing need to shake her off.

'You're looking good, Matheo. We hear your new company is doing well.'

Her heavily made-up eyes swept over him. Was that an undercurrent of wistfulness? *Envy?*

'I'm very well. Hard work suits me.'

'Evidently. Your father will be surprised to see you. We hear you don't like leaving St Celeste these days.'

He flexed his shoulders. 'It's possible to work remotely. I have all the resources I need to run the business from there.'

She ran a pointed nail down his sleeve, slanting a look up at him.

'But surely it must be lonely?'

So that was where this was going. She was digging.

He glanced towards Cassandra. Her head was thrown back as she laughed at some comment her companion had made. The flawless amethyst glittered against her equally flawless skin as she put a long-fingered hand on the man's arm and turned towards Matheo.

A few strides would bring him to her side, but he held back, keeping his cool. She came towards him, lilac silk swishing softly around her hips, her eyes sparkling with amusement.

'Matheo, I must introduce you…'

The words died on her lips. Confusion flashed in her eyes as she saw Claudia. For a second her step faltered. He was sure he only noticed because he was so absolutely attuned to her every movement. Her eyes engaged with his and he read a question in their depths.

Who is this?

There was a subtle change in her demeanour. Her smile became formal, her eyes watchful.

'Matt, let me introduce you to Kristof.'

Matt. The intimacy of the abbreviation of his name slammed into his chest, almost robbing him of the ability to breathe. He put out his hand to greet the older man, shooting him a direct look.

Hands off.

'Kristof. It's been a while.' His gaze shifted back to Cassandra. 'We've known each other a long time. Watch him. He's a devil with women.'

Kristof threw back his head and laughed. 'A reputation I'm proud of, Matheo. But I've heard it said of you…'

'Forget what you've heard. I see you've met Cassandra.'

Kristof levelled a look at him.

'Yes. And *I* see you've thrown an exclusion zone all around her. I don't envy you trying to enforce it, my friend.'

He turned his full attention back to Cassandra, taking her hand in his and bowing low. His lips brushed her fingers.

'It has been a pleasure, *mademoiselle*, but I will leave you with Matheo. He's a tough guy to do business with. I wouldn't want to tangle with him on a personal level.'

He disappeared into the crowd.

'You could have introduced me, Matheo.' Claudia's voice was shrill, any sexy huskiness forgotten.

He turned to look at her, longing to slip an arm around Cassandra's waist. 'Ask your husband to introduce you. They're old friends.'

Claudia's eyes slid to Cassandra. 'Who's this? I thought you were alone…'

'Why would you think that? This is Cassandra.' He saw her chin lift a fraction and her jaw tighten and then she extended her right hand.

Claudia's narrowed gaze swept over her as she offered a perfunctory handshake. 'Nice necklace,' she said.

'Thank you.' Cassandra's response was cool. 'It's a family heirloom.'

'Your family? Or his?' She darted a look at Matheo.

Cassandra smiled. 'Mine, of course.'

Matheo saw her words find their mark as Claudia's light blue eyes registered satisfaction. *He hadn't bought it for her.* Maybe not, but he wished he had.

His attention was drawn to a movement behind Claudia, and he fielded a powerful kick of apprehension to the stomach as he saw his father approaching through the collection of everyone who was anyone in the hotel business. He lost the battle with his better self and slid his arm around Cassandra's waist.

Cassandra's pulse rate accelerated. Her heart began to thump against her ribcage. She breathed in, trying to concentrate on the flow of air deep into her lungs. It should have had a calming effect. But the exquisite touch of Matheo's hand on her naked back was the ultimate test. She'd have to work on refining her breathing technique. A frisson of sensation shivered through her as his hand slid around her waist, coming to rest on her hip.

She leaned into him and glanced up, seeing his gaze fixed on an approaching older man, and suddenly she understood. He was grey-haired and the hard planes of his once-handsome face had blurred with age, but she had not forgotten him. She slipped her hand over Matheo's.

'Matheo.' The accented voice was gravelly, accusing. 'We heard you weren't coming.'

'Never believe everything you hear.'

The man's gaze shifted to Cassandra, and his eyes narrowed. He raised his eyebrows in an unspoken question.

Cassandra put out her hand. 'How do you do? Cassandra Greenwood.'

There was a beat of silence.

'Joe Greenwood's daughter?' He swung round to face Matheo, anger twisting his features. 'What the hell are you doing with her?'

'We're working together on the Hideaway project,' he said calmly. 'Not that it has anything to do with you.'

Cassandra felt the heat of anger radiating from

him and she squeezed his fingers where they rested on her hip. Lines of fury deepened beside his mouth, and the urge to reach up and stroke them away was powerful. But she stood rigid in the iron-hard circle of his arm, pressing her hand over his.

'Not content with snatching the hotel from under my nose, you've taken possession of the contents as well,' Charles Chevalier sneered, his eyes raking over Cassandra, insultingly familiar. 'I suppose I should be proud of you, closing the deal *and* getting the girl thrown in. Did you, by any chance, get the family jewels too?' He laughed, but his eyes were narrowed.

Next to her, Cassandra felt a response to the jibe ripple through Matheo. The biceps of his arm pressing into her back bulged with tension and she was willing to bet his free hand was bunched into a fist. She had to stop him from using it.

The situation had to be defused somehow. She was almost sure Matheo would not hit his father, but he might say something that he'd regret, and which would damage his own reputation. She willed him to ignore his father's goading and walk away, but he stood still, his jaw clenched, his lips pressed together. Dark fire flashed in his eyes.

Cassandra turned towards him, dropping her eyelids, and then she stretched up on tiptoe and brushed her lips against his pale cheek, whispering in his ear. His arm around her flexed, then tightened, and surprise flickered across his face.

'Good evening.' He nodded curtly to his father and Claudia and began to steer Cassandra across the room towards the lifts.

She gripped his hand as if her life depended on it. If the look Claudia had given her was anything to go by, it probably did. As they made their way through the packed ballroom, Cassandra's only objective was to look like a couple whose sole intention was to get somewhere private as quickly as possible and tear each other's clothes off.

He punched the lift button. When the doors opened he drew her into the mirrored interior, keeping her clamped to his side.

Cassandra finally breathed out and turned to him, dropping her guard. 'They were surprised to see you. Did you know they'd be here?'

'He insulted you. He talked as if you were some asset that was thrown into the hotel sale. I wanted to punch him,' Matheo ground out the words furiously, pushing the fingers of his free hand through his hair, 'and I'm not a violent man.'

'I know you're not,' she responded softly, 'and anyway, how would that have helped?'

'It might have made me feel a hell of a lot better.'

'Maybe, but not for long. And then it would just have been fuel for the gossip columns. Can you imagine the headlines?'

She tried to disengage herself from Matheo's arm, but he tightened his hold, keeping her close. She felt a fierce strength in him, as if he was putting every ounce of his energy into holding himself together, and the reality of how difficult the past few hours had been for him hit her. She put her fingers to his cheek and felt him flinch. 'You can relax now. It's over,' she said, dropping her voice. 'I can go back to my room, and you can raid the minibar in your penthouse suite, if that's where you are.'

'I'm sorry your evening has ended so abruptly. You were enjoying yourself, before…'

'Yes, I was, but I was growing tired of chatting and fending off the odd bit of unwanted attention.'

'Thank you for coming to my rescue.'

'If *you* hadn't helped *me* earlier, I'd have fled back to my room, and *my* minibar would now be empty.'

'Does that make us equal, then?'

Cassandra smiled. 'Hardly.'

They may be cocooned together in this lift, but a chasm separated them. She looked up and their eyes collided, and locked, and the foundations of her belief in their differences shook. The thread that pulled them towards each other was stronger than all of their differences.

And that was the problem.

She was hyped up after the encounter in the ballroom far below, and she felt she was on the edge of giving in to a madness which, once tasted, would hold her in its grip for ever.

The rift between Matheo and his father was as wide and bitter as ever. Had his purchase of the Hideaway, which was meant to satisfy his need for revenge, been a waste of his money and time? And if that was true, would he remain embittered all of his life, allowing the corroding effects of his anger to destroy him? Her fragile sense of self-worth, so carefully built up, couldn't withstand such a negative force. It would destroy them both.

The lift glided to a stop and the doors opened, interrupting her racing thoughts, and Matheo stepped out with her.

'I'll…be fine, Matheo. Thank you for your support this evening…'

He shook his head.

'It is I who owe thanks. At least allow me to see you to your room.'

Cassandra dug in her clutch bag for her key card and Matheo took it from her fingers, swiping it so that the lock clicked open. She turned, feeling her smile wobble a little.

'Thank you.'

'So,' he said, running a finger along her jaw, 'when you said you needed to get back to your room, you didn't mean for me to accompany you?'

There was a teasing edge to his voice, but anger still burned in his eyes, and his mouth was stiff. She wondered, with a sudden swoop of her tummy, if he planned to return to the reception and continue the argument with his father. Surely he could see what a terrible idea that would be; the damage it would do. Perhaps, though, that was what his father wanted. Perhaps he was waiting for him to storm back into the ballroom and have a furious argument, or worse, in front of all those people and all those cameras. Any satisfaction Matheo had gained from buying the Hideaway would be turned to bitter shame and embarrassment. She needed to stop that from happening.

'If it will help you to relax, Matheo, I noticed a single malt in the minibar. Would you like to try it?'

He followed her into the room and the door clicked shut behind them. The curtains had been drawn across the wide windows, blocking out the deep sky, and the room was warm and dim, with just a pool of light coming from the bedside lamps.

Cassandra pointed towards the minibar.

'Please, help yourself. And I'll have a bottle of sparkling water.'

She perched on the edge of the small sofa. Matheo had poured the water into a glass for her, and she raised it to him.

'Here's to deciding not to punch your father, Matheo. Good decision.'

He sat on the chair at the desk and leaned forward, resting his elbows on his knees, one hand cradling his glass.

'I think you made the decision for me, Cassandra. Thank you.' He glanced across at her. 'And thank you for this. Otherwise by now I might have been back in the ballroom.'

'Mmm. That's what worried me. I assume Claudia is your father's partner.'

'Yes.' His eyes were fixed on the glass in his hand. Crystal facets sparkled with amber.

'And you don't like her.'

He sipped at his drink, then paused.

'No,' he finally said. 'I don't.'

'Have they been together a long time? She looks rather young.'

Matheo downed the inch of whisky in two swallows and placed the glass on the desk at his elbow.

'My father has had a string of women since my mother died. Claudia is the only one he has married.'

Cassandra thought about the loving, stable childhood she'd taken for granted until her mother had fallen ill, and her heart ached for Matheo and the insecure life he'd lived.

'I'm sorry, Matheo. So much of your childhood must have been confused and lonely.'

He laughed, without humour, the movement of his throat making Cassandra want to reach out and stroke away the tension.

'Yes. He sold the family home and after that I seemed to be sent to a different hotel, where he had a different woman on his arm, almost every school holiday. It was definitely confusing.'

'Perhaps he's settled down, now that he's found someone he wanted to marry. He might be angry about the Hideaway but maybe he'll let the old rivalries go if he's happy. You've done what you set out to do. Can you relax and let them go too?'

Cassandra held her breath. She longed for him to agree with her. She wanted to know that he could put his anger and desire for retribution behind him and move on. She'd seen the creative side of him, experienced his kindness and passion. He was so much more than simply a man retreating to his private island, being eaten up by anger and a need for revenge.

She watched as he scrubbed his hands over his face, dragged his fingers through his hair. His eyes were unfathomable when he stared at her again.

'Yes,' he muttered finally. 'Maybe. When I'm with you I feel different. Softer, somehow. More accepting of everything. I missed you, so much, when you left St Celeste. Your presence made everything better. I felt as if I could trust you, on every level. But I know trust is hard for you.' He shook his head and stood up. 'I should go. I've already said too much.' He sent her a half-smile.

'I'll send you into a panic and you'll run away, only we're already in your room…'

Cassandra's heart seemed to pause before launching into a drumbeat, which she was sure he must be able to hear. In the dim lighting of the room the planes of his face were shadowed and sombre, his eyes unreadable. He took a step towards the door.

She stood.

'Don't go, Matheo.' Emotion made her voice husky. 'Stay with me.' She reached him and placed the palms of her hands on his chest, feeling the beat of his heart through the crisp white cotton of his dress shirt. 'I've missed you too. I've thought about our kiss a million times, and I want you to kiss me again. If you think you can trust me, then I think I can trust you too. Only I can't trust you to go back to your penthouse and not be angry and sad, so stay with me.'

The shawl slipped from her shoulders, revealing the shoestring straps of her dress for the first time. He tried to control his jagged intake of breath, placing his hands over hers, trapping them against his chest.

'How can I relax when I'm alone with you? When your beauty and kindness steal my breath?' He brushed his lips across her forehead. 'But I don't want to stay—' he lifted his head and rested his cheek on her hair '—if this is simply a tactic to stop me from meeting my father and Claudia again. I'll only stay if you want me…if you *need* me…to be with you.'

He heard her breath hitch and she entwined her fingers through his.

'I want you to stay because I can't bear for you to go.'

He shrugged off his jacket and tossed it away, then allowed his hands to rest on the smooth, cool skin of her shoulders. Her breath quickened and the pulse at her neck fluttered beneath his fingers as he stroked his thumbs across her collarbones. The urge to crush her against him was overwhelmingly powerful but he fought against it, feeling the need to hold back, to treat her gently and with infinite care. The most precious thing in the world was held in his hands and he was so afraid of breaking it.

So he kissed her with restraint, trying to control the urgency that surged through his body, and then he dragged his mouth away from hers, breathing deeply.

'Cassandra,' he muttered, 'are you sure?'

'Matt.' Her answer was a sigh on an exhaled breath. 'Yes.' She lifted her hands and locked her fingers behind his head, pulling his mouth down and giving him full access to her own. He wrapped his arms around her, then hauled her against him, feeling her softness against his hard strength, tracing his fingers down her spine, eliciting little heated gasps of pleasure.

His big hands flattened against her shoulder blades, feeling them pull down as her body arched towards him. When he circled his fingers on a spot below her ribs, her head fell back and he moved one hand up to support it, sliding his fingers into her hair. As his control began to slip, he brought his mouth down hard, onto hers.

Then his fingers slid to the silk straps of her dress and eased them off her shoulders.

Her gown shimmered to the floor in a lustrous pool of silk. His hands spanned her narrow hips as his eyes travelled over her neat, rose-tipped breasts, the half-moon indent of her navel and the long, long length of her legs. Then he put an arm behind her knees and the other around her shoulders and swept her feet from the floor. Her face dropped to his neck as he carried her to the bed.

CHAPTER FOURTEEN

FOR THE THIRD morning in a row Cassandra woke from what felt like a drugged sleep, her consciousness surfacing with reluctance through layers of satiated overindulgence. Parts of her ached with an unfamiliar but pleasurable hurt and a sensitised tenderness, but, as her mind began to catch up with her body and her eyes adjusted to the dim light, the ache in her chest swelled, overwhelming all the others.

It was the best feeling in the world.

She'd had three wild, uninhibited nights with a man she was supposed to detest, and who was meant to feel the same way about her. They'd discovered they were both wrong.

She turned her head. He lay on his back, his body totally relaxed in sleep. She reached out and ran her fingers along his shadowed jaw, down the strong column of his throat. Then she rolled over and curled into his side, resting her hand on the sprinkling of dark hair across his chest and feeling the steady, reassuring rhythm of his heart. Already she wanted it all again, more slowly, so she could savour every second, store it away somewhere safe, to be remembered over and over in the future.

His thick, dark hair flopped over his forehead, and she brushed it away with a stroke of her fingers and dropped a kiss onto his temple.

In his arms she felt utterly safe, secure. She'd surrendered her trust to him and let him take care of her, just as she'd wanted him to, all those years ago.

Spending time with him on St Celeste had enabled her to get past his guard a little. She'd come to enjoy his flashes of humour and admire his fierce intelligence and his belief in what was right.

In his arms she'd bared her soul to him; allowed him to see her at her most vulnerable and open, stripped of all restraint or reserve. He'd repaid her trust with infinite tenderness and gentle consideration, putting her needs before his own but allowing her to push him beyond the barriers of his self-control before they fell asleep in each other's arms.

The depth of trust, of emotion, had transcended anything Cassandra had ever experienced. The tight ball of anxiety and grief, which had become a permanent part of her, had dissolved under Matheo's hands and the sweet words he'd whispered to her as she'd unravelled in his arms.

This, she thought, is how it is supposed to be.

'Hey.' She propped her head in a hand and ran a finger across his lips.

'Hey back.' His eyes, heavy-lidded, opened, revealing smoky desire in their depths.

'I'm going for a swim. When I come back, we can…'

'We can what?' His voice was gravelly with sleep.

'Make love again? Maybe?'

'Mmm. Maybe? Why not now?'

He reached for her but she moved away, sliding out of the wide bed.

'Because now I'm going for a swim. But when I come back…'

'I'll order breakfast for when you come back, on my terrace. I need to replenish my energy.'

Cassandra bent over him and dropped a kiss onto his mouth, deftly dodging the arm that tried to capture her to pull her back into bed.

'Have another half an hour of sleep, Matt.'

'Mmm. You've worn me out.'

She slipped into the ensuite and pulled on her bikini and a beach wrap and left the room, closing the door quietly behind her.

The infinity pool was almost deserted at such an early hour. On the far side, one swimmer ploughed up and down, getting in his daily exercise. The rays of the low sun were already warm on her back as she slid into the cool water and felt the instant joy of being immersed in it. She swam, unaware of the time or distance, until her muscles ached slightly and she'd become out of breath.

Then she stretched out on a sunbed to dry off and recover her breath, closing her eyes against the sun.

She felt rather than saw someone near her. Her heart gave a bump at the thought it might be Matheo, but when she raised her lids she saw brightly painted toenails on tanned feet next to her sunbed. Throwing her arm across her face to shield her eyes from the sun, she sat up.

Claudia, in a gold bikini and oversized sunglasses, gazed down at her.

'Swimming on your own? Where's Matheo?'

Cassandra's brain, still engaged in her swim, struggled to change speed. But she thought quickly enough to decide that Claudia did not need to know precisely where Matheo was.

'I imagine he's asleep,' she said, lifting her hair and twisting it in her hands to squeeze the excess water from it.

'He didn't introduce us properly the other night.' Claudia hitched up the straps of her bikini top. 'He should have shown more respect for his stepmother.' She pushed her sunglasses onto the top of her head, revealing her light blue eyes, locked onto Cassandra's face. 'Especially since, until two years ago, I was *his* wife.'

A dull roar in Cassandra's brain eclipsed the morning sounds of the hotel. She shook her head, trying to clear it, and finally found her voice. *'What?'* But the single word came out as a rasping whisper. She felt her heart begin to race as adrenaline poured into her bloodstream. She struggled to stand up, scrabbling for her beach wrap with hands that shook. She clutched it around her shoulders, suddenly feeling terribly cold. 'I don't… No, I don't believe you,' she stammered. 'You're just trying to cause trouble. That's a… wicked…thing to say.'

'Oops.' Claudia clapped a theatrical hand to her mouth. 'So sorry. It's true, though. Ask Matheo. Or should I say Matt? He won't deny it, since he's so picky about honesty. Strange that he's never told you.'

Nausea rose into Cassandra's throat, and she was suddenly desperately afraid she'd be sick in front of this woman. She pressed a fist against her mouth and stumbled away, not sure how she'd find her way back to her room through the blinding tears which had begun to spill down her cheeks.

She slammed her room door and leaned against it, palms flat on the hard surface. Then she sprinted for the bathroom.

Long minutes later, she rinsed her mouth and splashed her face with cold water. Her eyes were swollen and red, her lips puffy. The pain that clutched at her heart was almost unbearable, but she knew she had to find the strength, somewhere, to get away, before Matheo came searching for her.

The thought of ever facing him again felt impossible.

Shame spiked through her at the way she'd betrayed the memories of her parents and of the long line of ancestors who had hung on to the Hideaway, through good times and bad. Not only had she let their most bitter enemy get possession of it, but she'd also…*trusted*…him.

Something inside her had changed and it could never be changed back. She'd glimpsed a side to Matheo she wouldn't have believed existed: thoughtful, intelligent and…*gentle.* Away from the cut-throat world of mega-deals and takeovers, where he came across as remote and ruthless, he was a different person. Her opinion of him had changed, and feelings for him which she'd have believed impossible a few weeks ago had slid quietly into her heart.

He'd held her in his arms as if she was the most precious thing in the world to him, whispering words that made her blush as she remembered them. He'd been gentle, at least at first… But he'd responded unfailingly to her needs and desires, which, she thought, the heat in her face intensifying, she'd made very, very clear.

But it had all been a lie. He'd let her trust him

with her deepest, most fragile emotions. She'd bared her soul to him, but he'd kept a shocking secret from her.

It didn't take long to pack. Anything in Matheo's penthouse suite could stay there. She'd never wear any of these clothes again. The memories and hurt they would carry would be too painful to bear.

Then she saw her key card to Matheo's door lying on the console table. Sliding it into her pocket alongside her own, she put down her bag and changed her mind.

From where she stood in the hallway of the penthouse, she could see him. He'd put on board shorts and followed through on his promise of breakfast. The table where he sat on the terrace held an array of covered dishes and a silver coffee pot. His stern profile was etched against the deep blue of the sky, his thick hair lifted from his forehead by the slight breeze, ever-present at this height above the sea.

Pain wrenched at her, and she had to resist the need to double over to ease it. The thought that she could pretend she didn't know occurred to her, but she dismissed it before it could even form properly. She knew she could never be that dishonest. One look at her and he'd know, anyway.

She had to confront him; let him know what she thought of him. Then she had to get as far away from him as possible in the shortest possible time. It would have been easier to simply disappear and let him work out what had happened for himself, but she'd made a split-second decision to face him, and she knew it was the right one.

As she watched, Matheo stretched his arms above his head, ran a hand through his hair and glanced down at his watch, brows drawing together. He must be wondering where she was. Taking a huge breath, she walked through the open-plan living space and stepped out onto the terrace.

Matheo looked up, his rare, heartbreaking smile lighting his face. Cassandra wanted to run to him, to wrap her arms around him, bury her face in his neck, breathe in his scent and let him tell her it wasn't true. But as he rose from his chair, his smile fading, her last shred of hope disintegrated. She could see, in those few seconds, that he understood what had happened.

'What's wrong, Cass?'

He moved towards her, but she put out a hand and he stopped.

'I saw Claudia by the pool. I think you know what's happened.'

His eyes, dark with anger, burned in a face from which all colour had drained. His chest rose on an unsteady breath and he put a hand on the table at his hip.

'I'm sorry, Cass.' He pulled his other hand

down over his face, shaking his head. 'I was going to tell you, but… I thought they'd left.'

A hot tide of anger swept through her and she did not try to curb it. Her hurt and shock would come back later, she knew, but right now, to do what she had to do, she needed to be furious. She folded her arms across her chest and stared at him.

'Exactly when? *When* did you plan to tell me, Matheo? Because I think you've had loads of opportunities. So many that not using one of them looks suspiciously deliberate to me. And when you thought they'd left, did that mean you also thought you were out of danger? That I wouldn't find out, so that made it okay?'

'I… We were… I was afraid…' He dropped his head.

'Afraid of what? That I'd be shocked? You're right about that. I am shocked. But what shocks me most is that I let you deceive me. You're a Chevalier, after all. I should never have believed anything you said.' She sucked in a breath, trying to steady herself but feeling the iron grip she'd tried to impose on her emotions beginning to slip. 'I *trusted* you. And you let me, but it was all a lie. I tried to help you overcome your anger at your father and Claudia and you…let me. You… made love to me. Was it to block out memories of…*her*? Is that all it was? All it's been, these last three days? Has it even *worked*?'

His face, when he raised his head, was ashen.

'No, Cass. Believe me. It wasn't…it isn't…like that.'

'Like what, Matheo? Because I can't see what else it can be like. You said she was your *step-mother*…you said you didn't *like* her…'

'I don't.'

'But you did once. Enough to marry her.'

'No. Yes, I mean, yes, I did marry her. But it wasn't that kind of marriage.'

'Just how many different kinds of marriage are there, Matheo?'

'It was…two powerful families. Money played a part… I never wanted to be married. God knows, the example of my parents' marriage was hardly a recommendation. But it was convenient, and our families had been hoping it would happen since we were children. At first it was okay. Even good. But then…'

'This is the twenty-first century, not the Middle Ages. I'm afraid I just don't believe you. But if what you say is true, I understand why your father behaved as if I was some sort of bonus thrown into the sale of the Hideaway to sweeten the buyer. You pretended to be up-to-date outraged, but it's just the medieval way your family has always behaved.'

'No, I don't suppose you do believe me, and that's not surprising. But,' he said, his eyes capturing hers and holding her gaze, 'the only thing

I do want you to believe is that I never intended to hurt you. I would have told you. I just needed…'

'The time to have told me, Matheo, was when I invited you into my room after I'd met your father and your…stepmother…at the gala reception. Yes, I would have been shocked. I mean, how the hell did something like that happen? But I would have listened, and I would have cared about how you felt.' Her voice cracked on a half-sob, and she swallowed, swiping the back of her hand across her cheeks. 'But deliberately deceiving me was unforgiveable. Pretending you cared for me…'

'I wasn't pretending.'

'But you let me give all of myself to you while you withheld something from me. You said you trusted me and that helped me to trust you. But you didn't trust me enough to share something so important with me. My trust has been wasted, shattered. You were just another man, telling me what he wanted me to hear to get what he wanted.'

Cassandra spun round, bunching her fists, and began to walk away. Matheo lunged after her, grabbing her by the arm.

'Cassandra, please, wait. I can explain…'

She shook his hand off. 'There's nothing left to explain, Matheo. I'm leaving now. Please don't follow me and please don't try to contact me, ever. I'll complete the Hideaway project, but I refuse to interact with you, on any level. I cannot work with someone who is so utterly selfish.' She walked across the marble floor to the door, sheer willpower keeping her upright.

'Cassandra...' She heard his voice crack, and her heart cracked with it, but she kept going. 'At least,' he shouted, sounding like a drowning man calling for help, one last time, 'now you know why the...*rift*...can never, ever be mended.'

That stopped her. She turned and stared at him across the space.

'Un-mended, the rift between you and your father will ensure that you remain a bitter, lonely and solitary man, so I suggest you find a way to repair it.' Her hand fluttered to cover her heart. '*This* rift...the one between us...*this* is the one which will never, ever heal.'

She wrapped both her shaking hands around the gold doorknob and yanked the heavy door open. It closed behind her with a muted click. There was no going back. She'd left the key card inside.

The tight band of pain around Matheo's chest tugged even tighter. He tried to slow down his breathing, to control the shake in his hands, but nothing seemed to work. He stared through the penthouse suite towards the door, hoping...hoping for what? That she'd come back? That was never going to happen. She'd said, quite clearly, that she wanted nothing to do with him, ever again. And why would she? Why would any woman?

What woman would want a man whose wife had left him for his father, thirty years his senior? What did that say about him? Did Cassandra think he'd wanted her not only to blot out the appalling fact of Claudia and his father being together, but also to repair the shattering blow he'd suffered to his masculinity? If so, she'd feel doubly used.

He felt physically sick at the thought of what he'd lost through his own stupidity, his lack of courage. He'd been desperate to tell her the truth. But every time he thought he could, he'd failed. Because the hurt and anger that slammed into him, when he had to acknowledge, to himself or to others, what had happened to him, terrified him with its destructive power. He couldn't bear the thought of how she'd react: the look of shock, her quick withdrawal, her retreat from him. Worst of all, the *pity*.

Anger kept him going, drove him to greater financial achievements, kept the reality of who he truly was at bay. Without it he'd crumble, have to face himself, admit he was an emotional failure and not worth anyone's love.

It had been a brutally painful experience. The betrayal of his wife had been compounded many times over by the complicit betrayal of his father. The pain he'd come to know—the twisting knife—flashed into his gut again. It was a match made in heaven, his father had stated, and, moreover, it was what his mother had said she wanted. He'd hoped they'd grow to love each other, that it would be all right, but he'd been wrong. Claudia had been in love with what she thought he could do for her, and when she saw his father could do more she'd easily made the switch.

His father had been delighted. He'd never been able to stop competing with the son who had stolen his wife's attention and love from the minute he was born.

Matheo turned away and walked to the edge of the terrace. The view, which he'd been looking forward to sharing with Cassandra over breakfast, was blighted. He resented the sun for continuing to shine in the cloudless, cerulean sky, the sailing boat skimming over the sparkling sea far below. He buried his face in his hands, trying to obliterate the image of Cassandra's tear-stained devastation.

He wanted to take her face between his hands and kiss away her sadness; tell her she was wrong about him. He was nothing like his father. The need to hold her, to keep her with him, was overwhelming. Without her he would simply cease to function.

He had to stop her from leaving. It would take her time to pack, to get a taxi. There might still be time.

He dragged on a shirt, raked his fingers through his hair and sprinted for the lifts.

Reaching Cassandra's floor, he looked up and down the empty corridor, then jogged towards her room. The floor concierge stepped out of his discreetly hidden office and Matheo stopped in front of him. He raised his hands, wanting to seize him by the lapels in his desperation for information, but politeness got the better of him and he dropped them to his sides, clenching his fists. The man's expression quickly changed from startled to polite helpfulness.

'Have you seen Mademoiselle Greenwood this morning?'

The man nodded and looked at his watch.

'Yes, sir, I have. She asked me to call a taxi to the airport for her.'

Matheo pinched the bridge of his nose between his thumb and forefinger, breathing and praying for patience. 'When was this?'

'Fifteen minutes ago, sir.' The man glanced down into the atrium. 'She seemed to be pressed for time. She'll be on her way by now.'

Matheo's heart plummeted. She'd either been ready to leave before she'd confronted him, or she'd left without any of her possessions.

'Did she say where to? Did she have luggage?'

He shook his head. 'Just the airport, sir, with her luggage. I assumed she was late for a flight.'

Matheo rested his hands on his hips. He dipped

his head, looking at the floor, and realised he hadn't put on any shoes. Dubai was an international hub. Hundreds of flights departed its airport for destinations around the world every day. Cassandra could be on her way to anywhere in the world.

'If there is anything more I can do for *monsieur*…?'

He shook his head.

'No, thank you. There's nothing anyone can do. I've screwed up. Big-time.'

He walked blindly back to the lifts and punched the button. Thin, silver-tipped fingers grasped his sleeve.

Turning his head, he looked down into Claudia's cold-as-ice eyes.

'Matt,' she purred. 'Is everything all right?'

'Don't call me Matt,' he snapped. 'And what does it look like?'

'Oh, dear. Sorry! I thought that was the endearment *du jour*. What's happened to the poor girl made good?'

'I don't think you need to ask me that question.'

'Ah. Trouble in paradise. Well, if you need a shoulder…'

'I'll never need a shoulder badly enough to need yours, Claudia.'

He stepped into the lift, closing the doors on whatever she was going to say next, and returned to the echoing emptiness of the penthouse. Grabbing his phone, he swore as his shaking fingers stumbled over the screen. But then he found her name and made the call. It went straight to voicemail. He clicked it off without leaving a message and tossed the phone aside. She was gone.

Panic clawed at him, stealing his breath and bringing him out in a cold sweat. He couldn't bear the thought that she'd gone for good. He'd held her, kissed her, stroked her, cradled her and soothed her when she'd cried out his name, over and over.

Matt, Matt, please…

He shook his head violently, trying to dispel the memory of her voice, her willing, supple body, her generosity. How was he ever going to get through the next hour, the next day, never mind the rest of his life, without her? No one else had ever called him Matt. Now no one ever could.

He sat on the end of the bed and pressed his fingers into his temples. He couldn't believe she could walk away from what they had; what they'd shared. He'd got to know her; experienced her kindness, her concern for others. He'd never meet anyone else who would spend their trust fund on paying the employees of a doomed hotel.

Then he thought about what he hadn't told her, and he could easily believe she could abandon it all.

He'd let her trust him, but the fear of revealing his true self had meant he'd been unable to be honest with her in return. She was justified in feeling betrayed.

He needed to find her to say sorry. To promise it could be different; that she'd never need to doubt him, ever again.

But then he remembered her parting words. She wouldn't listen to him or speak to him. And he couldn't blame her.

He needed her back, to tell her that what they had shared was fragile and irreplaceable. To tell her he'd wanted her, and her alone, and that the thought of how he'd hurt her was intolerable. He needed to tell her they'd stopped the clocks, changed the projected course of their histories. Together, the two of them could end the feud that had ripped their families apart for a century.

But he knew she never wanted to hear what he needed to say.

The vast marble halls of the airport hummed with life, and Cassandra plunged into the crowds, no longer looking over her shoulder, wondering if he'd come after her. She bit down on her bottom lip, walking fast to the departure gate, praying the flight wouldn't be delayed, keeping going until she was settled in her seat.

The big aircraft lifted into the warm air, banking over the sea. She leaned her forehead against the cool window glass and watched as the massive structure of the hotel came into view below them, standing tall on its own island, glinting gold and white in the bright sunlight.

She felt she had to press her hands over her heart to keep it from shattering. This couldn't be—she couldn't let three days define her life from now on. She thought she'd learned from Jason never to trust a man again. Her faith in her own judgement had been strong, but Matheo had slipped past her defences. She'd have to rebuild them, stronger than before. But as the hotel disappeared from view and all she could see was the shadow of the plane skittering over the waves far below, she knew she was leaving a part of her behind that she could never hope to get back.

Looking back was useless, she told herself. Yesterday was over and each new day meant she had the rest of her life ahead of her. But whatever all the tomorrows might bring, none of them would ever match up to the yesterdays with Matheo.

CHAPTER FIFTEEN

THE FIRST CLEARANCE his pilot had been able to get was in the early hours of the morning and now the journey, which Matheo usually enjoyed, seemed interminable. He downed the couple of inches of whisky that remained in the tumbler at his elbow and swore under his breath. He knew he shouldn't be drinking at this time of the day. His hand scraped over his unshaven jaw.

He'd tried to feel angry with her. When Claudia had left him for his father, he'd been almost blind with rage. An all-consuming need for revenge had followed soon afterwards.

He'd never felt like this. This sense of loss was unfathomable, and it had not lessened over the past two months. He refused to admit the thought that Cassandra might have gone for ever.

He'd left Dubai and withdrawn to St Celeste. He'd spoken to Nick, giving him free rein to carry on with the Hideaway project, but asking for regular, detailed updates on progress.

He hadn't mentioned Cassandra, but, towards the end of their conversation, Nick had.

'Cassandra,' he'd said, 'is prepared to complete her role in the project, providing she has no direct contact with you. Are you on board with that?'

'Yes,' had been his curt reply, forestalling any further discussion on the matter.

It didn't stop him thinking about her. He imagined he saw her footprints in the sand on the beach. One night, a trick of the light convinced him she was dancing at the water's edge. His chef requested a few days' holiday as the food he prepared was going to waste.

The project would be completed in December and after that there'd be no way to know where she was or what she was doing. The thought was unbearable. He had promised not to contact her, but he had to at least try to speak to her. There were things that had to be said and only he could say them. He'd made a decision and he wanted her to know.

At Heathrow he strode off the jet with the briefest nod to his pilot and crew. The doorman of the Mayfair hotel where he kept a suite received the same minimal acknowledgement. He resented the minutes it took for him to shower and change, and then he took the lift to the basement car park and slid behind the wheel of his sleek convertible. The engine purred into life and the wheels squealed on the concrete as he headed out into the London traffic. He had the FuturePlan office in his sights.

The receptionist looked up from her keyboard with a practised smile as he pushed through the glass doors.

'Good morning. How can I help you?'

'I need to see Miss Greenwood. Urgently.' He dragged a hand over the back of his neck. His hair still felt damp. 'Please,' he added, as an afterthought. Now that he was here, he was desperate to get this done.

'I'm sorry,' she said, 'Miss Greenwood isn't in today. But Nick Jones is in his office…'

'Then I'd like to see him, please.'

The girl nodded and lifted her phone. 'Your name, sir?'

'Matheo Chevalier,' he said over his shoulder as he headed towards the lift.

'Top floor, turn left out of the lift, sir.'

Nick Jones stood with his back to the panoramic view, evidently forewarned by the receptionist.

'Nick.' Matheo extended a hand.

Nick shook it. 'I wasn't expecting you…'

'No, and I apologise for intruding without notice. I need to see Miss Greenwood. Where is she?'

'She's on a routine site visit to the Hideaway. That fact is in the progress report I emailed you this morning.'

Matheo's shoulders dropped. He'd worked himself up to this, not giving himself time to think about how Cassandra would react to seeing him. It had never occurred to him that she might not even be here.

'I flew in early this morning.' He pulled a hand over his face, realising he'd forgotten to shave. Again. 'I haven't checked my emails.'

'Well,' said Nick, calmly, 'it's perhaps just as well she isn't here since she doesn't want to interact with you. Coffee?'

'Please.' Matheo threw himself into the chair Nick indicated. 'I'm aware of that, of course. But I need to talk to her. Just for a few minutes.'

'You could call her.' Nick moved to the coffee machine in the corner and then carried a cup over to Matheo, who took it and shook his head.

'She wouldn't pick up. I know that without even trying.'

Nick put his own coffee cup on his desk and sat down. 'She's returning tomorrow afternoon if you want to come back. But I will feel duty-bound to let her know to expect you.'

Matheo downed his coffee and replaced the cup on the saucer. It rattled slightly.

'How long,' he asked, 'will it take me to drive down there?'

Nick shrugged. 'Five hours?'

From the door, Matheo looked back.

'Please, Nick, give me a head start? Make up an excuse. Say something came up and you forgot. Just please don't warn her that I'm coming. I mean her no harm. I just have to talk to her and if she knows I'm coming, she might...' He shrugged. 'She'll probably leave.'

The look Nick returned was steady.

'Okay. It seems to me you've screwed this up once already and perhaps you deserve another chance. Just don't screw it up again.'

Autumn had made landfall in Cornwall. Golden leaves fluttered from the trees in a cool, brisk brcczc, which ruffled the surface of the sea. The call of seagulls wheeling over the bay blended into the steady background track of the surf rolling into the cove. The waves had cast off their summer gentleness and rose and crashed onto the sand with purpose.

Cassandra picked her way over the rocks at the end of the beach until she reached her favourite one to sit on. She pulled up her legs and rested her chin on her knees. She could sit here for hours, listening to the hypnotic thrust and wash of the sea against the rocks. Behind her, the Hideaway crouched on the cliff, its windows blank and sightless without the softening frame of curtains or blinds. The sound of sporadic hammering drifted down towards her. The last few slates of the renewed roof were being fixed in position, making the ancient building weathertight once more. She could almost feel nostalgic about her leaky attic bedroom, now that the rain could no longer find its way in.

The building works were almost complete and the interior decorators had swept in, working quickly against the deadline of early December. It would be finished on time, and in time for the grand opening, which the PR team for Marine Developments had planned.

Cassandra still felt conflicted about the role she had played in the transformation of her home. She supposed a part of her would always long for its old, worn comfort, the familiarity of things never changing. But the new version of the Hideaway was stunning. The early ideas that she and Matheo had discussed on St Celeste had mostly been incorporated, with huge success. They had given the hotel a brand-new lease of life, which would carry it through the decades to come.

She could *think* of Matheo's name now, although she'd never spoken it again. Saying it out loud might shatter the brittle shell she'd constructed around herself over the past months, and if that cracked, all of her pain would spill out, beyond her control, for the world to see.

After her site visit, on her way through the gardens, she'd stopped to talk to George. The old walled garden had been restored and planted with fruit and vegetables, protected from the salt-laden wind by the high stone walls, and he was puffed up with pride.

'It's what I always wanted to do, Cassandra,' he said, his arm sweeping out in a gesture that encompassed neat rows of sprouting winter vegetables, espaliered fruit and a long glasshouse, built against the south-facing wall. 'Mr Chevalier has given me a most generous budget. Most generous.' His kind eyes studied her and she glanced away, afraid of what he might see in her face. 'Now, I know there's been bad feeling between your two families, but it seems to me he's a good man. Been good to the staff, too.'

She was pleased to hear he'd kept his side of the deal.

On her return to London she'd explained to Nick that they'd had a 'disagreement' and that she wanted no direct contact with him. Nick had listened, and not asked any awkward questions.

It had proved to be surprisingly easy to avoid him. He'd said he was happy for the project to progress and would be available for any urgent discussions or decisions. And then he'd allowed FuturePlan to get on with it.

There would be a couple more site visits she'd need to make and then there'd be the grand opening. In January she would start work on a new project and put the whole of her past behind her.

Waves splashed noisily onto the rocks near her feet, so she didn't hear his approach. She whipped her head round as a dislodged pebble plopped into a tidal pool. She scrambled to her feet, her back to the sea, narrowing her eyes against the low sun.

He hadn't shaved lately. His dark hair was rumpled and lifted from his forehead in the wind. Adrenaline set her heart banging against her ribs. Every muscle in her body tensed, ready to flee, but there was nowhere to go, unless she retreated into the icy sea.

He stepped over the rocks, keeping his eyes on her face, and stopped in front of her. A movement made her look down and she saw his hands clenching and unclenching at his sides. The look in his eyes said she wasn't going anywhere.

'Let me past, please.'

His eyes moved over her, as if he was intent on devouring every detail of her face and body. He shook his head.

'No. Not until you've listened to what I have to say.'

'Nothing you can say will interest me at all.' The wobble in her voice annoyed her, as did the shiver which raced over her skin, beneath the fleece she wore.

He nodded. 'Maybe. But I'm not asking you to be interested. I'm only asking you to listen.'

A strand of her hair blew across her face. She flicked it away. 'No…'

He crossed his arms over his chest, his knuckles white under the tanned skin of his hands.

'I've come a long way to speak to you, Cassandra. Please give me five minutes of your time. Then, if it's what you want, I'll leave and never bother you again.'

Cassandra stared at him and he dropped his eyes, but not before she'd seen the anguish burning in their obsidian depths. Against her will, it tugged at something deep inside her. He was hurting and he needed to talk to someone.

That feeling had been familiar to her since she was sixteen.

Short of pushing past him, there was no escape. She gave a quick nod and lifted her chin.

Relief flickered briefly across his face. The faint lines between his brows were more pronounced than she remembered. There was no sign of the almost-dimple.

He shoved a hand through his hair.

'I'm sorry.'

'No doubt you are.' Her voice was cool. 'Did you hope I'd never find out? That whatever it was you had with me would finish when we left Dubai and you'd never have to tell me? And if I'd found out later, from someone else, it wouldn't matter, because you'd have moved on?'

'No. That's not how it was. I wanted to tell you, that first night in your room. I knew I needed to, but…'

'But that would have ruined the atmosphere? I would have asked you to leave, instead of asking you to share my bed?'

'No,' he repeated. 'I knew I needed to, but I was too afraid.'

'Afraid I'd be…shocked?'

'I knew you'd be shocked. That was a given.' He sucked in an impeded breath and she saw how difficult this was for him. 'No, I was too afraid to show you who I really am. The man whose wife preferred his father. The man whose father thought it was okay to marry her. The man who couldn't talk about it because the depth of his anger and shame scares him.'

'I held nothing back from you. I was no threat. Yet you thought it was fine to take all I gave but not truly give yourself back. You said I could trust you, knowing exactly how difficult that was for me, but you weren't prepared to trust me in return.'

'I'm deeply sorry, Cassandra, for the terrible hurt I caused you. I betrayed your trust and I'll never forgive myself for that.'

'You speak as if it were all in the past. That kind of hurt might never heal.'

She bit her lip, trying to stop it from trembling.

'I'm appalled by what I did; by the damage I caused. When I held you, it felt as if I'd won the lottery and been able to choose the most precious thing in the world, and I chose you. How could I have destroyed that? I would give anything to be able to mend it, but I'll understand if you feel that's impossible.'

Cassandra glanced around at the beach where

they'd stood in the freezing water, almost kissing; at the hotel on the cliffs above, which had been the cause of all this; at the squat tower of the little stone church on the headland, where her parents lay, and felt sorrow wrap around her like a heavy cloak.

'I don't think it can be mended. The cracks would always show, and they'd break apart eventually. The pressure of your toxic relationship with your father would be too much. You'd still be an angry, vengeful man and I'd be the person trying to smooth it over, make you feel better, compromising myself. I'm sorry, too. But I just can't do that.'

A muscle in his jaw ticked, and he frowned.

'I know now how it feels to be different. With you, the anger loosens inside me. Your kindness and generosity are contagious. You make me a better, nicer person, the person I want to be.'

'I can't be that mirror, reflecting the person you'd like to be. You'll have to find a way to become that, from within yourself.'

He nodded. 'I understand I can't ask that of you. So I've found another way. I'm going to start with forgiving my father.'

Cassandra watched him turn and stride away over the rocks, then leap down onto the sand and make his way to the foot of the cliff path. The stiff set of his broad shoulders radiated determination as he began to climb towards the skyline.

CHAPTER SIXTEEN

THE MARINE DEVELOPMENTS PR team had arrived at the Hideaway like a whirlwind. All the public rooms had been decorated for Christmas and the scent of cinnamon, citrus and pine hung in the air.

Three decorated Christmas trees, the golden angels on their tops brushing the newly painted ceilings, graced the hall, the drawing room and the dining room. The bannisters of the staircases sported garlands of ivy, interwoven with tiny lights, and arrangements of creamy, scented narcissi, red holly berries, bay leaves and spruce stood on tables. Candles were grouped on every surface.

Producing the celebration buffet in the dining room had been a valuable test for the new kitchen team and serving it had stretched the just-trained waiting staff to the limit, but there'd been no disasters.

At least, none that Cassandra had seen.

Puddings wreathed in blue flames had been carried in, accompanied by cheers and applause, and the whole event had finished with the pop of Christmas crackers.

The guests, many of whom had booked to stay for the weekend, drifted away to enjoy tea in the drawing room.

Cassandra slipped away from the festivities. She'd debated whether to come but, in the end, felt she owed it to the staff, especially Tess, to be there, and the temptation to experience the Hideaway decorated for Christmas and filled with people enjoying themselves was too strong to resist. This was how she'd be able to remember it, and she felt grateful for that.

She'd dressed up for the occasion in a green velvet dress embellished with delicate gold embroidery. The fabric swirled softly in a full skirt from a pointed dropped waist. It made her feel ethereal and medieval, as if she came from an earlier incarnation of the Hideaway.

The study remained her favourite room. The stonework of the ancient fireplace had been cleaned and repaired and a warm fire flickered in the grate. Around it the oak panelling had survived, stripped of centuries of dirt and smoke and polished to a deep shine. The once grimy walls had been painted in a soft shade of grey. The wide floorboards gleamed, a perfect foil for the intricate pattern of a Persian rug of ruby, sapphire and pearl wool.

The mullioned panes in the deep bay where she

stood were softened by heavy linen curtains in a shade of rich cream. Her old desk faced the view and a lit lamp cast a soft glow on its oak surface. Some of her favourite pictures hung on the walls.

The pale light was fading fast over the cove, transforming the sea from winter blue to deep indigo. She'd wait for full darkness to fall, and then she'd leave.

To her intense relief, Matheo had not come to the party.

Two weeks after their last meeting, she'd had a message from him.

It's done.

It had been two days before she could make herself reply.

What happened?

You don't need to know, but it feels good.

I'm glad.

Then, two days later, when she'd had time to think it through, she'd sent:

Do you need to talk?

No, thank you.

That had been his reply. She'd heard no more from him. It was over.

'Will it rain tonight, do you think?'

Cassandra stiffened and a frisson of sensation prickled across her scalp and down her spine. The atmosphere in the room shifted subtly and she wondered, briefly, if she'd conjured up a ghost. His voice was dark, and very familiar.

'The wind has changed direction,' she said, 'and there's a weather front on the horizon. We won't see the sun again until tomorrow.'

'How do you know what the sun will do?'

He was behind her now. If she turned, would he disappear? Her breath moved to her throat, and her pulse quickened.

'You said you didn't want to talk.'

'I didn't. I wanted to see you.'

Cassandra turned. He took up more space in the low-ceilinged room than she remembered. Slim black jeans and a soft black V-necked sweater defined his powerful thighs and wide shoulders.

'You're not dressed for a party.'

'I haven't come for the party. And anyway, you make up for it. You look…you are…beautiful.'

'Thank you. The hotel looks amazing, don't you think?'

'I haven't looked. I'm here to see you.' He moved to stand next to her. 'I want to tell you about my father.'

Cassandra nodded. 'Okay. Do you still feel good?'

'Yes. Better each day. I went to see him after we spoke.' He glanced towards the beach. 'It wasn't…easy. We both shouted.'

'Nothing too horrible, I hope.'

One corner of his stern mouth lifted. 'No. I accused him of never stopping competing with me. Of neglecting my mother. Of being overbearing and a bully. Of betrayal.'

'All true, I think.'

He nodded. 'Yes. But he pointed out that, from the minute I was born, my mother's attention… and *love*…was focused on me. He felt excluded. The only way he could attract her notice was by behaving badly. I'd never seen it from that perspective.'

'That doesn't excuse his behaviour towards you and your…wife.'

'Ex-wife. He accepts that. He said he knew his actions were unforgiveable. But I said I want to move on, that I'm done with arguing. We shook hands and I left.'

'It must have been difficult.'

'Of course; it wasn't as easy as it sounds. But I'm trying to find it in myself to forgive him, and I'm making progress.' His face was sombre in the soft light. 'The man I was with you is the one I want to be all the time. I don't expect you to want to be with me. As you said, the pressure on you would be intolerable. But I want you to know that I am trying to be that person. It was you who showed me how I could be, by believing me and trusting me, even though I didn't deserve it. I'd like to think that one day I might become the sort of man who could earn your trust, and your love.'

'Matt.' It was so long since she'd allowed his name to cross her lips that it felt odd. She put out a hand and rested it on the soft jumper, feeling his racing heart and knowing how hard this must be for him. He'd learned from childhood to keep his feelings hidden, his emotions in check. He'd suffered loss, he'd feared and then despised his own father, been betrayed by him and his wife. And yet he was willing to try to change, for her sake. 'Matt,' she said, again, 'you're incredibly brave. I know how afraid you are of trusting anyone. This must be terrifying for you.'

'Yes.' He nodded. 'It is. But I can do it if I think of how you trusted me, when I know how frightening that was for you too.'

A shiver of emotion shook Cassandra. Matheo put his hands on her shoulders.

'You're cold.'

She shook her head, breathing in deep, shaky gulps.

'It's not cold.' Her teeth chattered. 'The new eco-friendly heating works beautifully.' She gave him a shaky smile. 'It's...emotion. I wasn't prepared for this, but… I regretted the things I said to you when I left you. I was so shaken, so broken, but I should have let you speak. I was terrified you'd persuade me to stay, because I wanted you so much, but I knew I had to go if I was to have a chance of surviving as myself.'

He slid his hands down her arms and linked his hands with hers, pulling her towards him.

'If it's what you want, Cass, I will *never* let you go again. Not ever.'

He loosened his grip on her hands and smoothed a stray strand of hair off her cheek, pressing his lips to her forehead.

'Oh, Matt, it's what I want, but I'm so afraid of it.'

'Let me help you to build your trust in me. Allowing me to love and trust you is a way of allowing yourself to love and trust me.'

He wrapped his arms around her and she buried her face in his chest, inhaling his familiar scent, absorbing his strength, and feeling that need to allow him to shoulder her cares, to look after her.

His lips hovered close to hers. As if in anticipation, the tip of her tongue touched her top lip. She felt his chest rise sharply, pressing against hers. Her eyelids fluttered up and the grey depths of his eyes swamped her. His fingers speared into her hair, and he cupped her head in his hands.

'There is a culture,' she said softly, 'with a tradition of mending broken porcelain with molten gold, rather than trying to hide the cracks. The repaired object is regarded as more beautiful than the original, and much stronger, too.' She took a quick breath, seeing the silver flames which ignited in his eyes. 'If we can mend each other so that our relationship is shot through with gold, we'll be strong enough to face anything together.'

His deep, slow kiss was what she'd been longing for. He cupped her face and angled her head to ease her lips apart under his. Her hands moved from his shoulders, and she tangled her fingers in his hair, pulling him down to her, revelling in the feel of his hard body. She surrendered to the erotic slide of his tongue against hers, and to the deep sound of desire that came from his throat. His hands left her face and drifted down, leaving a burning trail of need in their wake.

When they broke the kiss, to drag air into their lungs, Cassandra ran her hands over his broad chest.

'Have you seen the rest of the hotel?' she murmured. 'I'd like to show you around.'

'Mmm. Yes. But there's something I want to show you here first.'

He placed his hand on her back and urged her towards the fireplace. On the hearth stood an ancient wooden chest, bound in rusted iron.

'I've never seen this before. What's it doing here?'

'I had it brought from its temporary home in a bank vault. At some point I thought I'd find you in this room, and I wanted you to see it.'

'But what *is* it?' Her eyes flew wide.

'The builders working on repairing the chimney caused part of it to collapse. They found this in the rubble. It had been built into a cavity in the brickwork. Are you going to open it?'

Cassandra knelt and gripped the iron hasp between her fingers. The rusty hinges creaked as she raised the lid, releasing the faint scent of sandalwood.

The glitter of gold, threaded through with rubies, sapphires and emeralds, gleamed against the dark wood. Ropes of lustrous pearls lay in thick coils among the jewels. A coronet of diamonds rested on a velvet cushion.

'This is what my father and grandfather *really* wanted. They had scant interest in a failing hotel, but a lot of interest in the rumour, which persisted down the centuries, of the Chevalier treasure my escaping ancestors had brought with them from France in 1789.' He shook his head. 'Generations of people have searched for it. Most people had discounted it as a legend, as I think you had. At auction, the contents of this old chest will more than replenish your trust fund. You'll be free to do exactly as you please.'

'Dance in the sea…?'

He nodded.

'Fasten my hair with a pencil?'

'Of course.' His voice was quiet. 'If that's what you want.'

'But, Matt, there's only one thing I want.'

He raised an eyebrow at her. 'Which is?'

'I want to be with you,' she said. 'I want to be able to love you without restraint, and I want you to love me back.'

He knelt beside her and pulled her close, flattening his hands over her shoulder blades, smoothing his palms down her back.

'That's what I want, too,' he said, his voice muffled against her hair. 'But there's one thing in there that I'd like you to keep.' His tone became grave. 'If you want it.'

He closed his fingers around something in the box and then opened his hand. The amethyst in the ring that lay in his palm sparkled with gentian fire. Diamonds surrounded the purple gem, creating a rainbow halo of light.

She drew in a long, long breath. 'It's the most exquisite, beautiful thing. It's so delicate yet its light shines so brightly.'

'It reminds me of you,' he murmured. 'Delicate, yet your light shines strong and true. And you're the most beautiful thing I've ever seen.' He dipped his head to rest his forehead against hers. 'You've shown me the importance of honesty and trust and that I'm capable of loving you so deeply that I know I'll never, ever stop.' She turned her head and rested a cheek against his chest. His heartbeat was as steadfast as his embrace. 'We'll be together, whatever the future holds,' he said, 'starting tonight.'

'Oh, Matt. I'm afraid I have to leave. I'm getting the train back to London. All the rooms here are booked for tonight.'

He nodded. 'Yes,' he said, 'they are. And one of the master suites happens to be in my name.' He gripped her hand in his. 'Let me show you.'

* * * * *